Tony Plumb
and the
Moles of Ellodian

Tony Plumb

and the

Moles
of
Ellodian

JM SMITH

Matador
9 Priory Business Park,
Wistow Road, Kibworth Beauchamp,
Leicestershire. LE8 0RX
Tel: 0116 279 2299
Email: books@troubador.co.uk
Web: www.troubador.co.uk/matador
Twitter: @matadorbooks

ISBN 978 1789015 034

British Library Cataloguing in Publication Data.
A catalogue record for this book is available from the British Library.

Printed and bound by CPI Group (UK) Ltd, Croydon, CR0 4YY
Typeset in 11pt Minion Pro by Troubador Publishing Ltd, Leicester, UK

Matador is an imprint of Troubador Publishing Ltd

To Sandie Byrne

One

Tony Plumb couldn't avoid looking at the wall, spotted as it was, with sticky tape. One poster's tackiness had outlived the others, it loomed big and bright and fibbed.

A True Home
for Children
with Difficulties

Behind the zingy orange text, Tony could make out a faded image; an assortment of grinning children, running in a garden. Standing to one side were two smiling adults and a dog.

Ellie clicked by on her way to her desk at Evensham Social Services reception. 'All right, Tony?'

There's the smell, what is it today? Hmm, quite nice, a mixture of chewing gum, washing powder and oranges, maybe banana? No, it's oranges. Ellie, Ellie, flowery Ellie, sweet and oh so smelly.

Tony flicked his balled-up bus ticket into a bin.

In fact, thinking back, it's been a series of 'homes', each one more dreadful than the last. Red Roofs, Fair Acres, Daisy Bank. It seems the cooler the name, the worse it's been. A True Home for Children with Difficulties, more like A Truly Difficult Home for Children.

Tony rubbed his nose.

I seem to have been waiting in this foyer forever. These chairs are beyond lumpy and those funny-shaped stains look like a Rorschach test. My psychologist would've had a field day. Will someone please come along soon and tell me where I'm going next?

Tony sighed. *Who exactly am I waiting for this time?*

Uncrumpling the letter she'd sent, he re-read her name. Ms Bendy Leggett.

She'll be dippy and all she'll talk about's her cat, just like all the others. It says here that we've met before. When? Hmm, apparently when I was five.

He couldn't remember that.

Ms Bendy Leggett might have made this up, just to get me on her side. Then again, all that stuff happened when I was five, like parents dying. Well that's what they'd said, but maybe I'm part of a spy thriller where Mum and Dad have been smuggled away to a place where they're safe, probably abroad. If not, and they're right and my parents really are dead, then they'll be ghosts who'll wait 'til the coast's clear and come back from the other world, to find me. My psychologist said it's OK to think these things if it helps, but I don't see that one anymore. Some adults

will tell you anything, and I've got to be careful. Bendy.
Bendy Leggett. Hang on, I know her, well I remember
her. Staff at Daisy Bank said it was someone called
Bendy who'd sorted out McGurney, my African Grey. I
must have made my point, because staff finally got the
message that a bird, not just any bird, but a parrot, **that**
magical parrot, was going to make it alright when things
got out of hand, and he did. Just thinking he was there
calmed me down. McGurney aside, Daisy Bank was the
last place and the worst place ever, but I think Bendy
Leggett's probably OK.

He looked at his shoes and up to the doorway,
where the social worker would eventually appear.

Then again, while finding me a parrot was excellent,
where was Bendy when I got stuck in a shower cubicle
and nobody heard me shouting for one whole hour? And
where was she when that horrible beetle-eyed, so-called
carer pushed me into…

Tony shivered as dark thoughts circled like hungry
vultures, waiting to tear at his mind.

It's been ten minutes. That Leggett woman can go and
boil her care plan. I might as well just go.

Heading for the door he collided with a short,
curly-haired young woman wearing a yellow scarf, a big
smile and carrying a buff-coloured folder.

'Tony Jones?' she said, holding out her hand, 'I'm
Bendy.'

'My name's Plumb, not Jones.'

'Of course, my mistake, Tony Plumb.'

3

He followed Bendy to an alcove off the waiting room, where she pointed to a plastic chair by a desk and the interview began.

———∞∞∞———

'So, Tony, I think I've told you everything, that's about it, that's the plan. Have you got any questions?'

He had predicted she'd say 'any questions'. Every professional said 'any questions', but only answered certain questions. His face began to redden and he almost used a word that up until quite recently would have meant a Daisy Bank detention.

'I see I've been in care too long.'

'I'm sorry Tony, what do you mean?'

'Any questions? Yes please, I have, they're the same questions I always ask. Does anyone really know what happened to my mum and dad? And how come I've been in care since I was five, but no one's ever wanted to foster me? How come I don't know, even simple stuff about myself?'

'I'm sorry Tony...?'

Tony twisted his face away, tears glinting.

'No need to tell me, I already know – it's for my own good. Better keep this little ginger-haired boy in the dark, in case he flips out.' A tear dampened his cheek and looking at his shoes again, he jerked his shoulder away from Bendy's hand.

Bendy said she had to make a phone call. Tony

watched the clock.

And now I'm feeling all bad because I lost it a bit. Maybe I've frightened her off? Hope not. Is she coming back? This phone call's taking long enough. Here she comes. Wow, she's power walking. What's with all the rush? How come everything's moving fast? Why's she whispering? Weird, and why's she passed me an envelope under the desk?

His thoughts clung to chariots as they whirled around a bright, colourful arena. Trouble was he didn't feel like he was in charge of the chariots, but then again, did he ever?

'You'll be OK at the new place, I'm sure,' said Bendy.

Another new place and how does she know I'll be OK? I suppose she does have a nice smile. Anyway, the plan sounds cool because anywhere's better than Daisy Bank.

Tony glanced down at the envelope. A sheet of paper with some squiggly lines poked out.

That looks like a map.

'Cheerio then,' said Bendy, leaning over to hiss into his ear, 'I might not see you again before you go.'

Why all the secrecy? There'd been a lot of that at Daisy Bank. He shoved the envelope into his rucksack as Bendy hurried away.

'Thanks for the parrot,' Tony shouted, as she went through some swing doors and disappeared.

5

Stopping for a moment as the doors closed behind her, Bendy froze.

'What parrot?'

———❦———

Six days later with Tony's psychological report in her hand, Bendy prepared for a meeting with Inspector Hector Blunt.

'Sorry,' she said as she met him in the foyer, 'there are no spare rooms and the canteen's closed for health and safety checks, so this'll have to do.' Bendy pressed a button to summon the lift.

'Meeting in a lift,' muttered the inspector, 'whatever next?'

'It's just that...' she waited for the doors to close behind a man in a pinstripe suit. 'It's just that, I've made some arrangements.' Her voice dropped to a whisper. 'I've met Tony and well, he's a very bright boy. He, er, needs more than we can provide, much more.' Her eyes scanned the inspector's face, searching for a sign that he might understand. 'I think to send him on to psychiatric care is going to...' She paused. 'It's not going to be the best chance he'll have...I've found somewhere better...'

'Better?'

'Yes, a special unit, he'll have a progressive experience at a sort of school. It's a unique place.' Bendy tried to smile.

'Like care?' said the inspector.

Ding-dong. Doors opening. There was no one there.

Ding-dong. Doors closing. Going up.

'No, as I said, it's a special place, with extras. It's a bit different, it offers more than other places, much more…not everyone can go…'

'Why not?' asked the inspector, leaning forward.

'It's very, very expensive,' said Bendy.

'Is that the only reason some people aren't admitted?'

Bendy drew a quick breath.

The inspector's brows knitted together, '…and the funding for this, er, plan has come from…?'

'Tony's had a raw deal, but this is going to be worth doing…he's in a dream, he's vulnerable which is hardly surprising, parents dead, dreadful circumstances, eight years in care, I needed to, I had to intervene. Can you understand? Boys like Tony, they sometimes get lost in the system…and often, the system lets them down…'

'So, where's the money come from to send him to this place?'

Turning away, Bendy's hopeful expression collapsed.

'Where?'

Ding-dong. Doors opening. A woman and a man carrying a child came aboard.

Inspector Blunt rocked on his feet while Bendy exchanged a few words with the mother before the family left on the next floor.

Ding-dong. Doors closing.

'Where's the money from?' pressed the inspector.

Drawing her mouth into a straight line, Bendy stared at the inspector for three whole floors; a clear, brown-eyed stare.

Inspector Blunt sighed, 'I'm retiring next year, and I agreed to this meeting because this boy's welfare is important, but I don't need a problem at this stage of the game. I'm about to close the file on this family so I'd appreciate an answer. You want the best for the boy, so do I, but it needs to be fair and by jiminy it needs to be legal.'

A hankie appeared from her pocket and Bendy dabbed a tear.

'You must tell me Ms Leggett, you must.'

Screwing up the tissue in her fist, Bendy leaned in.

'And so, you tell me inspector, when was anything ever fair? And what does "fair" mean exactly?'

The lift wheezed to a stop, awaiting instructions.

'Look Ms Leggett, Bendy, I knew Daphne and Terry Jones for a long time before they died. During the last five years of their lives, my professional relationship with them was, well, intense you might say. Phoning me up they were, day and night, wanting news about their son who was snatched, y'know, the Victor Jones case; it's on your file I'm sure. It was hellish, I can tell you, for me and for them. Mind you,' he said, pulling himself up and frowning slightly, 'I didn't know they had young Tony staying with them, sort of permanently. I can't fathom how come nobody knew he was there?

Maybe between the police and social services we should have made more visits and been less keen to avoid their calls.'

'Hmm,' said Bendy. 'They must've been very good at hiding him, in the way only criminals know how; some tin pot notion that they needed a child to replace Victor, I shouldn't wonder. When neighbours were questioned they said they thought Tony was Daphne's nephew, but don't you see inspector, if you know what they were like, you must have some sympathy for Tony?'

Blunt looked at her sharply before his face softened. Ding-dong. Going down.

'Tony was stuck with the Joneses going through goodness knows what,' said Bendy. 'When I spoke with him, he said he couldn't talk to them because they were always drunk, out, or shouting. Apparently once, when he was about four, his mother fell asleep in bed with a cigarette, bad idea, and the duvet caught fire. Tony saw this happen. The bedroom was in flames, so his dad locked Tony in the loo. He doesn't remember the fire brigade coming but remembers being cold and crying in the bathroom; his dad shouting and throwing water, and then his dad threw cold water over him, over Tony.'

'He must have been terrified.'

'He was. Also, he still says his name's Plumb, not Jones.'

'Still says? Ms Leggett, have you met him before?'

'Sorry, should have said, yes, I have. He was first picked up by social services when he was five, after his parents' death. When Daphne and Terry Jones died, you know, the waterfall incident?'

'Of course. That was a terrible, terrible end. There's more to that than we first realised.' The inspector's eyes slid sideways. 'Still, they're dead, so any case against them is closed.'

Bendy nodded.

An uneasy silence hovered in the lift like a badgered ghost.

'He also remembered parties into the night and the police, the police came a lot.'

'I know about that,' said the inspector, 'I was there, reading the reports. A lot of improper behaviour.' He shook his head. 'They were arrested for possession of illegal drugs, almost every month. They didn't seem to care. As I recall, Terry did time at one point.'

'So, you see…'

'Well not really, Ms Leggett,' said the inspector. 'This story is, unfortunately, not unusual.'

'…My point is,' hissed Bendy, 'that Tony is…'

'What?'

'Unusual.'

'In what way unusual?'

Taking a breath, Bendy fished a typewritten sheet out of her bag.

'He's quite different to the usual type of teenager we see, he hasn't been spoiled by badness, if you know what I mean. He has a spark, he's bright and he has potential. Quite remarkable after what he's been through, and I haven't even begun to tell you what he says he experienced in care. Despite all he's been through, terrible troubles, I think he has a promising future.'

'Were there problems at the home?'

'You can say that again and not on Tony's part, poor mite,' said Bendy. 'The place has been closed down and I've lost count of how many staff are being interviewed. He was at Daisy Bank. There's a major investigation. Tony's temporarily accommodated somewhere else for now.'

The inspector groaned. 'I heard about that. I didn't know he was at Daisy Bank.'

Bendy nodded. 'And somehow, somewhere in all the kerfuffle he says he has acquired a parrot.'

'A parrot?'

'There are some mental health issues,' continued Bendy. 'The report says that he's emotionally very hard to reach. My reading of it is that Tony sometimes cuts off from what's going on around him, like he's behind glass or in a trance. It's more than just day dreaming. Oh, and apparently at times, he becomes psychotic.'

'Psychotic?'

'He loses touch with reality and lives in a world of his own.'

'Oh dear,' said the inspector. It was his turn to pull out a handkerchief. He caught the tear just as it left his chin.

Ding-dong. Doors opening. An elderly couple entered the lift. The man was in a wheelchair. Bendy and Blunt shuffled into a corner. The inspector tweaked the brim of his trilby and put the handkerchief back in his pocket.

Ding-dong. Doors closing.

The man in the wheelchair turned, as best he could, to Inspector Blunt.

'I never forget,' he said, pointing to his legs, 'there's always someone, somewhere who's worse off than meself. Kids in all sorts of scrapes and youngsters without homes. Terrible it is. They're the ones who need our help.'

Bendy smiled and Blunt undid the top button of his overcoat.

Ding-dong. Doors opening. The couple got out of the lift.

Ding-dong. Doors closing, going down.

'I've arranged the transfer to the new place. It's full board. He can stay there as long as he needs. The transfer has actually gone through.' Bendy bit her lip before muttering something that sounded to Blunt like 'no one's questioned it.'

Blunt leaned further in.

'Tell me how you arranged it,' he whispered, his eyes now damp and soft.

Pressing her lips together, Bendy bowed her head.

'How was it paid for?'

Standing up straight and squaring her shoulders, Bendy looked directly at the inspector.

'I moved some funds, without permission.'

'From?'

'An absolutely massive pot of dosh earmarked to rewrite all the county council's library stock of children's fairy stories, into politically correct versions of their former selves.'

A smile almost appeared on Inspector Blunt's face.

'That,' he said, 'shall go no further.' Glancing up as the lift doors opened, Blunt tweaked his trilby and stepped into the foyer.

Bendy let out a long, deep breath. As the lift doors closed she hoped the inspector meant that he would keep the confidence, and not that he would stop the transfer of one Tony Plumb to the new place, known by those in the know as Ellodian.

Two

'Do you have any brothers and sisters?' asked the fair-haired boy at the bus stop.

'No,' said Tony, 'I have McGurney instead.'

'Who's McGurney?'

'My parrot.'

'What sort of parrot?'

Tony looked carefully at the boy's blue eyes.

Hmm, they could be friendly eyes; maybe I could trust him.

'McGurney's a Congo African Grey parrot.'

'So, where is this parrot?'

'He's around, probably in a tree.'

''Course he is. Do you think I'm soft? You're the one whose parents jumped off the waterfall, aren't you?' said the boy.

'What waterfall?'

'Your parents were nuts. They jumped, everyone knows that. Nutty parents, nutty son.'

Tears gathered and threatened to spill, but Tony turned away and looked down the road for the bus.

'Your parents were bad 'uns, did y'know that? They smoked weird stuff and popped funny pills, leastways that's what everybody says at Daisy Bank. Did y'ever see them do it? Have you ever done it?'

Tony's face burned.

'Did yer? Have yer?'

'Of course not,' said Tony, scowling at the thought, but somehow this wasn't the answer the blue-eyed boy wanted. Unable to think of anything else to say, Tony pushed him away.

The boy ducked and rammed Tony, sending him backwards into a wall. Gasping, he clutched at his chest as the blue-eyed boy ran off, trailing in his wake unforgettable comments about Tony's mum and dad.

Trying to calm the contents of his mind by pressing on his ears proved futile. Mean authoritative voices, weaving about on thought chariots returned to skid and bump around his head, depositing memories wherever they pleased.

'We hope you'll be happy at Daisy Bank. Poor kid. You must miss your parents…Stop crying now and get on with dusting the ornaments…'

'Sorry there's no hot water for your shower today, cold will have to do…'

'No, no, no. Oh dear me no, madam, you misheard me, that little cupboard in the attic is for *toys*.'

'Oh yes officer, medication is kept to the bare minimum…'

'Now Tony, just keep quiet…you just trust me…I won't hurt you…'

'Ask no questions…hear no lies…'

His eyelids prickled and began to swell with tears. He remembered another time, sitting at the top of the stairs after lights out, overhearing a social worker telling another social worker something unpleasant about his mum and that his dad was worse.

'It's a mess,' they'd said.

Tony wiped away another tear.

The bus stop and the street came back into view. Loud fluttering in a nearby tree signalled McGurney's whereabouts. The parrot squawked, swooped and settled on Tony's rucksack. Managing to crack a smile, Tony fumbled in his pocket.

'Hello McGurney, good to see you. You seem to know when I'm sad. Have a peanut.'

Taking the peanut in his claw, the bird got busy.

Feeling calmer, Tony stroked the parrot's soft grey feathers. 'It's odd, y'know. I'm going to a special place, but do they mean special as in brilliantly good, or special as in – I'm doomed, and need all the help I can get? Bendy says there are people there who're older than me and people younger than me. I just hope there's somebody else at Ellodian who's thirteen and a half.'

McGurney blinked and carried on with his peanut.

'I mean, in the scheme of things, it's not really a

problem, well not after losing Mum and Dad. That was the worst problem. I s'ppose being packed off again, this time to Ellodian, with a few instructions and a map, is no big deal.'

McGurney wiped his beak on his claw.

'Bus's coming, McGurney, get in my rucksack.'

Climbing on board, Tony found a seat and opened the map. His thoughts drifted back to Bendy.

Funny, how she'd urged me to go. Practically shoved me out; hardly time to get all my stuff together. Anyhow Bendy's cool, Daisy Bank's over and I've got McGurney.

The edges of urban life slipped by and the town disappeared. Through the grimy window he could see trees and now and then, glimpses of a river. Tony kept his eyes on the landscape, noting a brown and white cow amongst a herd of Friesians, a church on a hill with a pointed steeple and a scrap heap in the corner of a field made up of rusting cars. To be on a bus, seeing new things and without a member of staff counting heads every ten minutes, thrilled him more than he could let himself believe.

According to this map...which way up...? I'm probably about a mile away from Ellodian. Better get off here, I think.

Tony jumped off, the doors closing behind him with a pneumatic sigh. *Wow, this countryside's big. Perhaps I've got off the bus too soon?* Further down the lane he could see an elderly man, ambling along with his dog.

'Excuse me.' The man stopped.

'Hello, d'you know where Ellodian is?'

Turning around slowly the man focussed and so did his dog. Both faces held a blank expression. The man sniffed and glanced at the ground. 'Never heard of it,' he said, 'what is it?'

'It's a special place, for people who are thirteen and other people as well. It's called Ellodian. They're expecting me. It's down by the river.'

'River's that way,' said the man pointing to an overgrown path, 'though, I doubt you'll find many teenagers down there.'

Tony thought quickly about how to describe a special place that helped improve the futures of everyone who attended.

'You must know it, it's probably like a college, the sort of place students might go, there'll be lots of people there...'

The man looked unconvinced.

A thought chariot with spiky wheels doinged off the inside of his skull.

'...people in gowns and big libraries and hopefully a scooter park, classrooms and a dining hall with cake and sandwiches and lots of...' Tony sighed, looked away from the man's cold stare and eyed up the narrow path edged with vicious nettles.

It can't be down there, can it?

The afternoon was warm, quiet and perfectly still. A tractor hummed in the next field, a bee buzzed by and the man didn't say any more.

'Right,' said Tony. 'Thanks.' Hoisting up his rucksack, he set off through the nettles and glancing back, caught sight of the man again.

He hasn't moved, he's watching me.

Striding out through the undergrowth, Tony headed down towards the river. Between the brisk thud, thud, of his step on the grassy earth, he could hear McGurney muttering peacefully somewhere in his rucksack. Finally, the man disappeared behind the brittle stalks of some old cow parsley, and Tony slowed down. Ahead, the river stretched out across the meadows.

OK, so…masses of trees, but no sign of Ellodian. Nothing other than a big, flat field. Well, it's got to be here somewhere.

He followed the curve of the river, stopping after ten minutes to take in his surroundings, his gaze sweeping the open fields for any indication of a building.

It's just completely flat. No sign of a car park. No sign of anything, full stop. According to this map, it should be here. The road's way back and I'm not even on the path anymore, this is just wall to wall greenery. The river's there, in front of me as clear as anything, but that's not on the map either.

'I'm totally lost.'

'You're quite right Prime Minister,' said McGurney, emerging from the rucksack to perch on Tony's shoulder.

The watery autumn sun slipped behind a row of oaks. Just ahead the river swooped to the right and there, through the dimming light, he could make out some shapes, the promise, possibly, of a welcoming place, a special place; his destination.

'That must be it.'

Breathless, he got to the structure just as twilight took the colour from the day and in disbelief, ran his fingers over the crumbly, damp, stone walls.

'Once a farmhouse McGurney, now a pile of rubble.'

Tony wandered around the mossy stones.

'Maybe there's a door somewhere.'

The trees and hedges darkened around him, morphing slowly into black lumpy shapes crouching silently in the cold open field. 'Who am I kidding? There's absolutely no way this has ever been a special place to help people.'

He kicked a stone.

'Well, I won't be needing this,' he said, crushing the map into a ball. He wanted to throw it into the river, but the terror of a Daisy Bank detention, even in its absence, still held sway. Tony stuffed the map into his rucksack while McGurney flapped and screamed.

'Quite right, quite right.'

The river swished past, chuckling and popping, and with it came sharp musical notes, drawn out from the evening air.

What's that?

Thin, melodic voices coming from nowhere in particular, wafted around him. Tony spun on his heels.

'Who's there?'

The noise of the river faded and his skin began to tingle as if someone with icy, wet fingertips just tickled the back of his neck. Breath visible in the chilled air, Tony shuddered as the atmosphere began to thicken and wrap around him like a damp itchy rug. Rubbing his clammy arms, he pulled a sweater from his rucksack and put it on. Darkness beckoned, the light faded and the air got colder still. As he flicked on his torch, something small and furry leapt beyond the cone of light.

There they were again, now forming words and sentences, tinny syllables chattering, gabbling and rolling towards him across the water. The talk got stronger, now sawing through the air, seeking out a target, moving closer, homing in. Quite distinct, the words swarmed up until – fwop – a sing-song voice spoke sharply in his ear.

'Trust me, I'm not going to do anything to hurt you...'

'Aaaargghh!' Tony lashed out at a speeding thought chariot, his torch beam raking the woodland like the headlights of a spinning car. 'Not her, not her!'

Memories rushed in of the beetle-eyed woman, her smelly armpits and that hungry expression, scuttling toward him with a sickly smile. Her voice pinged off the river, penetrating the heavy silence of the wood and splitting his mind into fragments; a psychic kaleidoscope but minus the symmetry, minus the pattern.

'...I'm not going to hurt you, you just trust me...'

'You ugly witch, you and your freaky ideas. Why won't you just let me go!'

'…Ask no questions, hear no lies…' she uttered.

'No! No! Go away, go away! You don't belong at Ellodian!'

A twig snapped close by.

'Go away! Leave me alone!'

Hauling up his bag, Tony staggered into the shrubbery, his tongue dry and his back wet with sweat. Pushing branches out of the way, he ducked to avoid the rebound of lashing stems, until – whoooosh – he slipped and tumbled down the bank towards the river.

'It'll be cold and wet…'

Tony screwed up his face and braced himself, but instead of crashing into the gurgling current, he felt himself falling, falling, falling.

—⟋⟍⟍—

He stirred to the sound of McGurney's fluttering wings.

Nursing a feeling that he'd chipped his skull and maybe lost a kneecap or two, Tony wondered for a moment if the wet patches on his legs were splashes from the river, or if the wetness was blood.

Calm, calm.

Pulling down his jumper, bunched up from the fall, he tried hard to stop trembling. Reaching out, his fingers sank into the damp, spongy walls and snatching a breath, the cold tang of sodden vegetation shot up his nose.

Smells like the garden at Daisy Bank after it's rained. At least now I've got my socks and shoes. Where am I?

Shapes and strange shadows gathered around, some moving, some still. Standing up carefully, he tested his knees, which although sore, held his weight.

The torch had landed on the soil floor a few feet away, casting long shadows in all directions. Ducking to avoid something solid overhead, he picked it up and shone the beam around. Above, a web of twisted wooden limbs hung down from a ceiling of soil. Great dollops of mud clung to the woody web, like flat black bats that had died a decade ago.

'It's like a cage. A cage of roots. I'm looking up at the roots of a tree.'

Droplets of water hung like insecure chandeliers, occasionally releasing a bauble that plopped down and splashed on the mulchy floor. Small pools collected in the cupped-out boughs of old creeper and jagged slabs of stone. The root cage fanned out around him, with openings big enough to climb through.

Attempting to dry his hand on some moss, which it turned out, was just as wet as the walls, Tony inched the torch over the pitted surface. 'Good boy,' he whispered to McGurney, 'stay quiet, something very unpleasant might be lurking.'

Through the openings, strange forms mushroomed up from the darkness. The torch trembled in sync with his hand, but there was no sign of the beetle-eyed woman. The beam hit the back wall, and as the light swung slowly across, a large black cavern yawned wide with a tongue of wetted debris pointing out the way.

'What's down there?'

Crawling out of the root cage, Tony found he could stand up.

'There's masses of room and look, there's a light.' Along the damp path, by a curve in the rock, a burning torch stuck out from the earthen wall. 'It's a corridor, some sort of passageway. McGurney! I'm here, I'm at Ellodian, and it's buried underground!'

About to take a step toward the flickering lights as they danced down the shadowy tunnel, he quickly froze. A voice shrieked out from somewhere very close. Wasting no time, Tony leapt behind a curtain of ivy, pressing back against the wall. Shaking, he tried to block out the cries.

'...But the moles have been here since medieval times...lose the portraits and I worry we'll lose the moles. We can't let the portraits go just because there's been another flood.'

'...But frankly, Headmistress, they do appear a little, well...damp,' said a calmer voice.

'Miss Frankly, you are correct in what you say, but these moles have built this institution. Their fathers, their grandfathers and their great-grandfathers, mothers, daughters and daughters' daughters.'

McGurney landed silently on a root by Tony's head.

'Moles?' Tony whispered. 'Bendy never said anything about moles, or that I'd be going underground.'

The bird tipped his head to one side and blinked his beady eyes.

'Yes, you're quite right, Prime Minister.' McGurney wasn't much good at whispering.

Taking a deep breath, Tony emerged and followed the sound of the voices, stopping abruptly when three adults in long grey gowns, two women and a man, came into view. They were peering at a row of paintings hanging on the walls.

Hiding again, this time behind the branches of a weeping willow, he peeked through the fronds.

Paintings, they're looking at paintings and they're all of moles. Moles! And they're dressed in proper clothes. How wacky is that?

The creatures wore builders' helmets and steel-capped boots, sat on scaffolding, ate sandwiches or pored over what appeared to be maps or plans. One or two larger portraits showed a single mole in a suit and tie.

Tony smiled. The moles were really cute.

'Er...er...four hundred and twenty-five, a lot, such a lot,' said the man whose gown swung around him as he circled on the spot. He spoke quietly, to no one in particular and had a soft pallid face. 'A lot, oh yes, a lot.' The larger woman, who had crimson hair, turned to the small, grey circling man.

'What's that, Prospect? Oh yes, I know what he's trying to say, Ellodian has employed the services of four hundred and twenty-five moles over the years, Miss Frankly, so it's pretty important, wouldn't you agree that these paintings stay right here, adorning this corridor?'

Miss Frankly, a thin woman clad in tweed and peering through round metal spectacles, gave a little nod. 'As a mere school elder, I bow to your judgement as headmistress, Mrs Sherbet, but would remind you that to restore the paintings when water has stained them, birds have nested behind them and more recently a pupil defiled them with graffiti, is not inexpensive.'

'Double negative,' muttered Prospect completing a circle. Mrs Sherbet and Miss Frankly ignored him.

'To be honest, Davinia,' said Mrs Sherbet, 'I couldn't give a whistling fig about keeping the portraits, but this sort of thing seems to mean something to people, you know, history, traditions, honour, recognition, that sort of gumpf. I can never see it myself, but there you go.'

'Frankly, er...I see,' said Miss Frankly, stiffening and looking a little shocked.

'Bser...er...ser,' said Prospect and started to turn around and around on the spot even quicker than before.

'Time to go, I think. Come along Deputy,' said Mrs Sherbet to Prospect. With that the headmistress and her deputy swept past, leaving Miss Frankly standing alone in the dimly lit corridor.

'Well, frankly,' she said, and hovered. Tony spied his chance.

'Hello, er, Miss Frankly? I'm Tony Plumb. I'm new. Can you tell me, where I'll – um – sleep please?'

'There's another boy just down the corridor who frankly, I think is asking the very same question. Why don't you find him?'

Casting his eyes to the floor under Miss Frankly's glare, his face hotted up and when he looked again, Miss Frankly had disappeared.

'Not very helpful,' he muttered and turned to find a small, shrinking boy.

'Are you new too?' Tony asked, studying him carefully. He'd got a lot of hair on his cheeks and his nose wobbled like jelly on a trolley.

The downy boy sniffed and inching closer extended his mobile snout. Tony shot a glance at the portraits and back to the boy, whose sniffing had become methodical, searching and almost invasive.

This boy's like a mole.

Tony took a step back.

'Hi, I'm Tony Plumb.'

'Gaskin.'

Suddenly a very tall man appeared, with leaves trapped in his hair. In his hands were two custard yellow crash helmets, complete with chin straps and two long, grey gowns.

'Put these on,' he barked, 'and no, you don't have to sleep in them.'

Tony pulled a face at Gaskin, but the mole-like boy gazed up at the tutor, his tiny eyes fixed in awe. Gaskin whispered 'Thank you,' and dutifully put on the helmet and the gown.

'Mrs Sherbet says visors down at all times.'

'Visors down,' repeated Gaskin, snapping his shut.

'Bedrooms that way.' A long bony finger emerged from the tutor's gown and pointed to one of several torch-lit corridors leading further underground. 'Assembly takes place every morning in the hall and of course, absolutely no talking to anyone, friends or students.'

With that he turned and strode off.

'My sense,' said Tony, trying to grasp hold of the situation, 'is that we've found ourselves deep inside a very spooky labyrinth.' He turned to Gaskin, but Gaskin had gone.

'Pull yer socks up, pull yer socks up,' said McGurney, hopping from one foot to the other.

'What d'you make of that McGurney? Weird, right? Hmm, as usual you're just giving me the old beady eye routine. OK, gown, helmet, rucksack. I s'ppose I'd better find my bedroom. Come on.'

Three

Being inside this crash helmet's a bit like being underwater. Being at Ellodian's totally about being underground. Underwater and underground.

Tony snorted.

Bendy must have some fantastic ideas about how being at Ellodian is going to help anyone who's just got out of care. No timetable's arrived or been pinned up anywhere and anyone I ask, just shrugs.

Trying not to stare, Tony sized up a couple of the other residents who wafted silently by.

Everyone's wearing those grey gowns, complete ankle ticklers, and yellow crash helmets with their visors down. They look like space-people; I can't tell boys from girls, or anything about anybody and this flickery torchlight doesn't help.

'Who…? Ouch, watch where you're going will you?'

Some students scampered by, pushing and shoving down the leafy root-lined corridors. Tony held his breath and leaned into the wall. A distant tapping noise reached his ears and got louder and louder, until five elderly people with walking-sticks came into view and shuffled by, leaning on their sticks and each other for support. Apart from the tapping, both groups were completely silent.

Were those racing youngsters human? They might be like Gaskin. Are there more moles than pensioners here, or more pensioners than moles? What if I'm the only real, human kid?

The air around his head got suddenly very cold and his breath billowed out in a thin white stream.

Maybe they're automatons and someone or something's controlling them. Am I here to be modified? Is there a baddie at Ellodian who wants me for an underground zombie? C'mon now, don't spook yourself, but guess what? I'll be leaving as soon as I can. There must be a door or exit I could slip through.

His thoughts were interrupted by a hollow thumping, signalling more traffic on its way.

Right, I'm in here.

Falling in step with a group of jogging students, clearly going somewhere, Tony tried to catch the eye of the person beside him.

'Where are you going, or – er – where are we going?'

A voice from inside the crash helmet shouted something that sounded like – MALE.

Male? Is this a cool new way of introduction? Is this how people meet at Ellodian?

Tony was about to yell 'male' back, when his fellow jogger jangled a sparkly bracelet.

Hesitating, Tony said nothing.

The group galloped on, turning right into the dining hall and out through a large door; no more than a gap in the bank that led out onto a pebbly shore and the river. Emerging through curtains of ivy and into the daylight, Tony came upon dozens of students, pushing their cloaks back and brandishing fishing nets. The river ahead was glassy, almost still and very swollen.

'Why have you got a fishing net?'

No one answered. Someone gave him a fish-eyed look.

Fanning out, some students jumped into the shallows, while others waded right in. Distracted by the organised way in which everyone seemed to apply themselves, Tony temporarily forgot about escape. No one was looking his way, the open fields, tawny and autumnal rolled all around and the river coursed past, but Tony stayed put and watched.

They're holding their fishing nets like they expect to catch something, but what? Somewhere a clock struck ten and suddenly dozens of tiny multi-coloured boats with names painted on their prows, came speeding down the river. The students swooped and flailed about in the water, fishing out their boat before hoisting themselves onto the bank. Then, like a flock of scattering doves, white envelopes fluttered everywhere.

'Letters,' whispered Tony.

The colourful boats shot past and he strained to read the name on every one.

I've missed mine, the river's too quick.

Further upstream he could make out a wooden building.

'What's that?' he asked a dripping someone, who stood close by. The person lifted their visor. It was a boy, who looked up from his letter and followed Tony's pointing finger.

'That's the House of Miniature Mail Boats,' he replied, eyeing the bank for a tutor, before shutting his visor and moving away.

He's worried about the no talking, visor down rules but I can hardly hear him anyway through these padded crash helmets. I need to get hold of a fishing net. If mail's coming in, then maybe mail's going out. Bendy might write to me here, and if she does, a letter could arrive any day saying I've been 'placed' somewhere else.

Gaskin, nose aquiver, came into visor vision and thrust a small boat into his hands before scampering off. The boat said 'Tony' on its side. He reached inside and pulled out a letter. It wasn't from Bendy.

Dear Tony Plumb,
    Welcome to Ellodian. You can try to escape if you want, but it's not worth it. You might as well stay and complete the following task.
    Your tutor is Prospect.

Your aim is to find answers to the following questions:

What happened to your mum and dad?

How come you've been in care since you were five?

Who are you?

You are now on course to start exploring stuff for yourself. Find out the truth Tony Plumb.

Yours Sincerely

Mrs Sherbet,

Headmistress.

PS. Remember, there is no escape from these questions. To shirk this duty is to sign up for a unidimensional life.

Escape? So, I'm a prisoner then?

He read the letter again.

*Hmm, maybe a prisoner to ignorance. No one's ever answered these questions even when I've asked, and I've asked them loads of times. Is it time to find out the truth? Do I really **want** to find out the truth? A unidimensional life – what does that mean?*

His mind, fighting the crushing weight of pounding thought chariots, struggled to revisit the ideas he'd considered, on and off, for a very long time. Just as he reached out for an idea, it was whisked away in a cloud of dust.

How come no one's told me what really happened to Mum and Dad? Is it my fault my parents died, and how'd they die anyway? That boy's comments at the bus stop; that was the first I've heard of a waterfall. That first question: What happened to your mum and dad, has got to include: How did they die? So, how did they die?

Thought chariots whizzed around his psychic arena, changing course and bumping about.

And how come I've been in care eight years? Why didn't I go into foster care like a lot of other kids did? Was I that bad? So bad and horrible that nobody wanted me?

The fact is, while Ellodian's truly bonkers, weird and escaping does hold appeal, there's something about being here that's sort of OK…Well, it isn't Daisy Bank for a start. And, if I do try to escape, I could end up somewhere worse, much worse.

He shoved the letter into his pocket.

What are the chances of Prospect being any help with this three-question quest? He seems a tad lightweight, but maybe he's got hidden depths? He seems harmless enough. I guess I'm going to find out. I just hope he'll be better than…

A tear pricked in his eye as the sun glittered on the water. Tony kicked a pebble into the river.

'Chuckle and pop,' he murmured.

Saying that had started with the other river, the river that ran near home. I used to say chuckle and pop when Mum and Dad were alive…before care…before they died.

34

Images began to gather in his mind, memories of when he was five years old.

Come to think of it, even when Mum and Dad were alive, I was alone. Chuckle and pop's the river voice that talked to me when I was lonely and fed up. I can't recall Mum and Dad ever playing with me, but the river was always there. Hmm, other kids weren't allowed anywhere near it. I s'ppose it was slippy near the deep bits, but even kids as old as six couldn't play there; I was only five and I could play there all day, and sometimes 'til past dark.

A frown scudded across his face.

When I was about four-ish, I remember other kids wanted to play, at least at first, but then a parent came out and dragged them off. Why was that? What did they know? Mum let me play by the river a lot while she sat on the sofa with Dad. When I got home, I had to be careful not to knock over their drinks, or the bottles, or step in the ashtray, or disturb them too much. Then there was that funny smell. Playing out was way better than staying in.

———⟊———

One summer, he recalled he'd scrambled down to the river's edge and crunched his way along a narrow shore of pebbles. He'd walked a while and the sun had sunk behind the trees.

Suddenly in the growing dimness, a bright dot had caught his eye.

There it was. A little boat, caught in the weed on the other side of the river. He could see a yellow patch on its side and maybe a pale blue cabin. Wanting to find out more, he'd waded in. Then, without warning, the riverbed gave way and down he went, sucked into deep, cold water. He'd fought, but the current flowed fast.

He'd yelled out, but no one came and he'd ceased to fight. A lightness came over him and like the little boat, he followed the will of the current, bobbing this way and that. Tumbling into the shallows he'd struggled to the bank and was emptying his boots and getting his breath, when he'd heard a man's voice.

'Are you all right there?'

It was Mr Burrow from the estate, walking his Pekingese. Tony's mum had said Mr Burrow was an atheist, which meant according to her, that in the eyes of The Blessed Pope, Mr Burrow cooked and ate children, pretty much every day.

'Yes, thanks,' said Tony, scrambling to his feet.

'I recognise you laddie.' Mr Burrow had begun to pick his way towards him, stepping over bumpy tree roots, holding on to branches and moving closer. Reaching out, the man made a grab for Tony's arm. He remembered how he'd out manoeuvred him by putting a tree between them, taking a quick step sideways and half hiding behind a shrub further down the bank. Mr Burrow had almost lost his balance and clung to a sapling. The Pekingese began to yap and Mr Burrow, finding better footing, bent down and picked it up. Tony scanned the opposite bank for signs of the boat but couldn't see it.

'What's your name?' he'd said.

'I saw a boat, a little one, with some yellow on it.'

'What's your name sonny?'

'Tony.'

'Tony what?'

'Tony Plumb.'

'Oh, Tony Plumb eh? Is that what you're called? I know you. You'd better be careful,' he said, glancing around, 'bad things can happen to kids when they're out alone.'

Mr Burrow turned, heaved himself and his dog back up the bank and walked away. Tony couldn't forget being sodden, cold and waiting until the child eater had gone before following the river home.

Sighing, he shook off the memory as the river came back into view. An idea bloomed.

I bet Mr Burrow's still alive and living on the estate. Maybe he could help me with the questions…?

'Oooooofffff!' He was on his knees with a sharp pain in his back.

'Hey, that hurt!'

'It's lunchtime, day dreamer,' said a gowned, yellow-helmeted someone.

Four

Standing in the suppertime queue a few weeks later, Tony found himself behind Prospect. Careful not to bat the tutor with his tray, he stared at his back and at the soft grey folds of the tutor's gown. The material looked warm and he wanted to touch it, just lightly, but his heart began to beat hard and his mouth dried up. Being so close to an adult who wasn't reading the riot act or asleep, felt new and sort of good.

'Only ten dabsters this year,' said Prospect to another tutor in front.

'Hmm, but still…not bad,' said his colleague, who Tony recognised as the tutor with leaves in his hair.

'It's as much as we can cater for,' said Prospect. 'As you well know, being such a small institution, our full complement of dabsters is thirty really, but…under the circumstances, we couldn't manage…Let us say we are full at twenty-nine. Then there are the friends of course.'

'Well I guess that's just the way things are,' said the colleague with a tight little smile. 'At least we have our jobs, twenty-nine students and the friends to help out.'

Tony paused as Prospect emitted a small sigh and hanging back, waited, as the tutor picked up a ladle and helped himself to the brown soup; apparently all there was to eat at Ellodian.

Ladling out some soup for himself, Tony took his supper to an empty corner of the dining hall, and went over what Prospect had said:

'It's as much as we can cater for you know…'

What did he mean? Room for thirty dabsters, is that the technical term for a student or a resident? Thirty students – but we have only twenty-nine? Where's the thirtieth student then?

It's a pretty funny set up. What really is a dabster and who are the friends? Prospect seemed busy, but not with tutoring, so what's Prospect doing? What plans had Ellodian for its dabsters?

Tony stared into his bowl and began to wonder if underground zombies were allowed to keep their brains.

Is it only me and that nervous, twitchy-nosed Gaskin who're waiting to be shown around? An introductory tour would be good, and some information.

The following morning at assembly, after everyone had sung Ellodian's special anthem 'Blue Suede Shoes', a student asked Prospect a question.

'When do we get our timetable?' The voice sounded female.

'A question young dabster, a question. You should refer this question to your tutor.'

'…But you are my tutor,' she said.

'Check that out with your tutor,' said Prospect, 'and you might put your visor down, yes, I think, yes.'

Assembly broke up.

'Excuse me,' said Tony, 'do you know who that girl is, the one who…?'

'Shhhh!'

'Erm, I'm looking for…Aaoooww!'

'Turn it off bird brain.'

Tony rubbed his freshly kicked shin. 'Are you the girl who…?'

'Shut up new boy, we don't talk at Ellodian!'

Five

No shrill alarm bell, no fluorescent lights buzzing on at dawn, nobody pulling off the bed clothes and yelling in his ear.

Tony sat up in bed in his small underground room.

'I'm getting used to this now, McGurney. Y'know at first, this room looked so much like the cupboards at Daisy Bank and the dreaded bathroom, it took me about a week to risk taking a shower. Do I smell OK now McGurney? At least here, the locks fasten on the inside, the water gets hot and I can get out and get dry when I want to. Coolio.'

McGurney held a peanut in his claw and cracked it open with his beak.

'It's good being on the top floor, with the outside world just there, through my little skylight. Poking around in the ceiling and making that hole was one of my better ideas. The sunshine will pour in, when it comes and if I'm still here. See McGurney, I can even stop the rain coming in with this umbrella. All I need to do is stand on my chair and we're waterproof.'

Peering out through the gap this morning, Tony could see a square-ish patch of pearly sky; marbled silver with slender clouds. As the clouds moved across the sky, the late autumn light dimmed and brightened in his room and bird song filtered in.

'You're quite good at imitating those birds.' said Tony.

In the corner, a seat of petrified wood with cupboards above it grew up from the earth, quite likely fashioned by a gang of energetic moles. The cupboards had doors made of leaves, sticks and dried mud. Electricity cables lay buried in the ivy and water came through a wooden pipe that ran down to a square stone sink. Below the sink a wooden cupboard helped mask the sour smell that sometimes rose up from the depths of Ellodian. By another wall sat a small wooden desk, with ivy clinging to its legs, like baggy green socks.

Done with his peanut, McGurney perched on a root growing out from the wall beside Tony's bed.

Unfolding the letter from Mrs Sherbet, Tony held it up to the parrot's face.

'I remembered Mr Burrow today, he might know something about this.'

The bird studied the paper and listened, his head cocked to one side, his eye particularly beady.

'Pull yer socks up.' McGurney moved along the root and then back again.

'This is all very odd, my friend.'

'Yes, you're quite right, Prime Minister.'

A glittery powder floated softly through the skylight, and onto the floor.

'Snow,' said Tony.

'Umbrella,' said McGurney.

Tony was about to question his parrot, who'd never said 'umbrella' before, when the little pile of snow gathered volume and began to move. His hand automatically flew to his head in an attempt to curb any unwanted thought chariots.

'McGurney, look...'

The snow moved again, and a little mole surfaced.

'Ooops sorry,' said the mole. 'I can usually tell where the bedrooms are y' know, they're much warmer than the rest of the earth, but this 'ere pile of snow, well it's confused me, that's what it's done, and I thought I was coming up outside, on the river bank like. I do beg your pardon sir, I'll be on my way.' The mole took a spotted handkerchief from his overall pocket, wiped the crumbs of earth from his nose and turned to disappear back down the hole.

'Er, Mister...' said Tony, pushing the snow aside with his hands and leaning over the little hole, 'Excuse me, are you still there?'

Muffled scrabbling ensued and in seconds the mole was back.

''Ello,' said the mole shaking the snow from his cap. 'Can I 'elp you?' He replaced his cap, tweaking the peak so it sat comfortably on his head.

'Erm, yes,' said Tony. 'I'm trying to find someone called Mr Burrow. I think he might be able to help me with something…er…some stuff from my past.'

'Is he a mole like?'

'No, but he walks his dog along the river bank.'

'DOG! Oh! My Giddy Aunt!' said the mole, stepping back and grabbing his overall bib with both paws.

'Sorry, the dog's quite little and its nose is so squished I doubt…'

'No more about dogs if you don't mind sir, please, no more.' The mole wiped his face with his hankie. 'I haven't 'eard of any Mr Burrow, but y'know our Princess Vicky has a lotta aides, servants and what not, but you won't mean her. She comes from London. Mole royalty like. I 'aven't 'eard anyone hereabouts talk of a Mr Burrow. Are you sure he's not a mole? The name's a bit familiar.'

'He's not a mole that's deffo, but he walks his, er, he walks along the riverbank. I thought you might have seen him.'

'Hmm, I don't rightly know if I can 'elp you after all sir. I'm sorry about that, but there you go, we can't be knowin' everything about everybody, now can we?' The mole chortled. 'A fine pickle we'd be in if we knew everythin' about everybody and there's no mistake. Folk need secrets.'

He turned to go but then pointed to the skylight.

'You want to get that hole in your ceiling sorted out sir, if you don't mind me sayin' so, or there'll be trouble again, if there's a flood like. Ellodian's had floods before.'

Tony shot a look at McGurney. *There must be some clue that might lead to Mr Burrow. Something, anything. Don't let the mole go!* Tony crawled towards the hole in the floor.

'Erm,' said Tony. The mole stopped halfway in, his head and shoulders above the bedroom floor.

'Was there something else?'

'Er, yes, there is.' Tony took a gulp of air. 'Do you think I could come to see you, and maybe well sort of visit, or something?'

'Oooh, now you're asking me,' said the mole, lifting his cap to scratch his head. 'I'll 'ave to ask me missus about that one. What sort of thing 'ad you in mind?'

'Erm, well,' said Tony, 'I've never been to a proper social gathering before, so maybe I'll come and say "Hello" and meet your wife? and maybe...erm...you could come back here?' He waved his arm around the room wildly; checking quickly how his room might appear through the eyes of the mole. 'Or I could take you out for an ice cream, or maybe some takeaway egg fu yung?'

'Egg fu yung...?'

'Yes, or maybe we could go to a movie...'

'A movie...y'mean like the pictures?'

'Exactly, or we could go for a walk...or do you like dancing? Have you ever been on a scooter? Scootering would be fab...'

The mole scratched his head again and gave a little chuckle. 'You certainly 'ave some ideas. Let me think about it, will you?'

Tony nodded. The mole waved and disappeared down the hole.

He listened as the mole's scrabbling got fainter and fainter and imagined him as a little power packed digger, tunnelling through the earth.

'No point going in for breakfast, McGurney, it'll only be brown soup and bread.' That was it. Every so often a bowl of fruit would appear but there was such a fight for it, a bloody scrum, that it was almost enough to make a case for wearing crash helmets. '…and in any case, we have to go.'

Foraging in his cupboard he found a bag of McGurney's walnuts.

Hmm, they're a bit green and these biscuits are all dry and crumbly. They'll have to do.

Slotting batteries into his torch, he slung on the only coat he possessed, found his scarf, filled his water bottle and set off to search for Mr Burrow.

Six

The common room – it's a start – there might be a notice board with clues and information.

He lifted his hand to open the door but a tutor popped his head out first.

'Due to river forces, rooms have moved eight feet down the corridor, this is my private lavatory and I would thank you to resist attempts to enter.'

Tony retreated quickly and tumbling into the next room along, spotted a pale rectangular space on the wall where a notice board might once have been. Peering closely at a tiny note pinned in the centre of the space, he read:

'Please note, the notice board is no longer here.'

A fishing net lay propped up against the wall. Snatching hold of the slender cane, he borrowed a pair of waders from the hallway and dashed out to look at the river.

It's quarter to ten and there's Prospect further upstream at the House of Miniature Mail Boats. The mail's on its way.

'Right, mister dithery,' said Tony, pulling on the waders, which were at least one size too big, 'I'll sort this out. If you're my tutor you've got to help me with my quest whilst I'm in this weirdo place. That, or if I'm lucky, I might fish out a letter from Mr Burrow explaining all I need to know about parents, childhood and everything – Hmm, slim chance, but I can only hope.'

The river was strong and coiled past the riverbank like a muscled, silver snake. Gowned and helmeted bodies entered the water. Tony waded in just as Prospect began shrieking and leaping about on the bank like an excited child. Tony jumped and almost lost his footing. It was as if Prospect had woken up and come alive.

'He's like a kid,' said Tony to someone who was preparing to wade in.

'Yes,' came the reply, barely audible through the visor, 'a kid that's never grown up.'

'Oooh, they're off!' Prospect screamed. He looked like some sort of mad pixie, dancing in his academic gowns and almost tumbling into the water, as he let loose a flotilla of tiny wooden boats that began to sail at speed downstream. Tony waded forward, feeling the pressure of the current on his knees. Mrs Sherbet stood on the bank with a loud hailer and a pair of opera glasses.

'Visor down,' she shouted sternly to another student who struggled to stay upright in the water. Tony snatched a quick look across the river.

That student might be Gaskin; it's so hard to tell.

The person floundered, trying to tug their uniform out of the reeds.

Whoever it is, they're just making the situation worse. They need help.

Distracted by a boat coming his way that said 'Mr B' on its side, he just glimpsed the person in the reeds topple, crash and sink completely under water.

At that moment, a boat with TONY painted in yellow letters on its prow, sailed past. Lurching forward, waders catching on the stones, he swiped and caught his boat. Lodging the prize down his jumper and steadying himself with rapid whirling movements of his arms, he turned to see the thrashing student in the reeds come up for air. With a howl and a thudding splash, the other lost their foothold again and plunged into the depths of the river, their helmet filling with water.

It's Gaskin, deffo Gaskin.

The small furry boy went under again.

No! he's going to drown.

'We need some help here,' shouted Tony, trying to heave his sodden gown out of the water so he could wave to Mrs Sherbet. Inside the helmet his face got hotter and hotter and his visor soon steamed up.

'Can you help us?' he yelled. Mrs Sherbet stood on the bank, silent and immobile.

Can she even hear me?

Locking his knees against the strong current and making his way to the side, Tony flung the fishing net and his boat onto the bank. Turning, he headed toward the drowning boy, pushing his coiling gown free as he waded out.

'He's still underwater, this is terrible, I'm about to drag a drowned boy out of the river.'

Tony tore off his helmet. 'Help needed, over here!' Plunging his arms in, the icy water shot up to his neck.

'A-argh! I-it's c-cold, m-my arms a-are f-freezin' off.' Trying to withstand the glacial needles, he grabbed hold of the floundering boy. Gaskin gulped a lungful as Tony dragged him clear of the deep current.

'Try to relax,' said Tony, his head banging against Gaskin's helmet, as the smaller boy wriggled and kicked, 'you're pulling me under too.'

Finding a good foothold on the riverbed, Tony tugged and hoisted the gasping Gaskin onto the riverbank.

'Take deep breaths, Gaskin,' said Tony.

Gaskin spat and choked, his small pink eyes shifting anxiously from Mrs Sherbet to Tony and back to Mrs Sherbet. The headmistress shouted out, her arms flailing about like a windsock in a cross-current.

Ree – lief, at last she'll organise some help.

Meanwhile Gaskin retched and coughed while Tony caught his breath. Numb with the weight of his cold, soaked clothes, Tony flopped back on the bank.

Gaskin's coughing subsided, and he wiped his downy face with a leaf.

'Put your helmets on,' Mrs Sherbet bellowed through the loud hailer as she stamped toward them. 'Put your helmets on at once, I say.'

Tony sat up. 'You have got to be joking! She cannot be serious.'

Beside him, Gaskin trembled uncontrollably, maybe from the chilly river water, maybe from fear.

'Thank you for saving me,' said Gaskin, dragging his wet robes around him.

'I can't believe what she just...'

But Gaskin had crawled through a side portal and back into the depths of Ellodian. Tony wrung out his cloak and was about to follow Gaskin when he spotted his boat, a few feet away and lying on the bank. Picking it up he opened the cabin and took out a small package.

What's this?

The outer wrapper, a waxed paper bag, was decorated with images of tall glass bottles like decanters, with pointy stoppers in red and orange and blue to show it came from a chemist. Peeling open the sticky tape he peered inside and pulled out a brightly coloured tube.

Is it toothpaste? The tube's a bit big.

HAND CREAM AND NAIL REVITALISER
PERFECT FOR THOSE CARE WORN HANDS.

'Er, why?' said Tony, out loud.

Seven

'Hey, amoeba brain, lunchtime's nearly over.'

Cold, shaky and dripping, Tony ignored the hissed greeting and stumbled into the dining hall. Stomach rumbling, he tried to find a seat. Hoping to remove his helmet, just enough to empty it of water, proved difficult.

'It's stuck, I'm trapped.' He tottered and swung about, trying to prise it off and then...Crunch!

Down he went, his legs whipped from under him, his wet, muddy gown folding around him like the wings of a crumpled bird.

'Hmm, almost glad of the crash helmet,' he muttered and tried to look around, but couldn't. His helmeted head had got trapped between a table and the wall. Straining, he could see his gown was caught on a rusty bolt sticking out of a table leg.

Someone rattled a teaspoon against a glass and the hall fell silent.

'Hello, is there anybody there?'

'Frankly,' said a familiar voice, 'I find it simply reassuring that after all my years at Ellodian, we have NOT bowed to the modernisers who have wanted us to remove the yellow helmet from Ellodian's uniform.' The dining hall remained silent and Miss Frankly continued.

'Frankly,' she said, 'this instance we have just had the misfortune to witness, and I mean here the tumbling of a boy, proves the necessity for the yellow helmet, irrefutably and without doubt. Frankly...'

'Thank you, Miss Frankly,' said Mrs Sherbet.

'Help me!'

A couple of faces popped into view overhead before retreating and Tony could just make out the muttering of a few senior staff, before silence resumed. He began to think he'd be trapped between the wall and the table forever, when it happened.

Two slim white arms reached down, and POP, off came the helmet and there, looking down from her chair, was a very pretty face.

'Hello,' she said, 'I think you could do with some help.' Tony gazed at the girl for a whole minute.

'Can you hear me?' She sounded concerned. Tony managed to sit up.

'Tony Plumb,' he said, 'Hi, how're you doin'?'

'Bobbi Appledown; you're on my foot.'

'Ooops, sorry,' said Tony, and managed to haul himself up onto the wooden bench beside her. Today the soup was on the table in a tureen, and Tony helped himself.

Bobbi gave him a little smile and Tony smiled back. He saw that Bobbi Appledown wasn't eating the standard brown soup like everyone else, but instead ate sandwiches from a takeaway carton, shoved in her bag.

Mmm, interesting, she's hidden her bag in those ferns so no one can see it.

Tony stole a glimpse at her face. It was as pink as a rose and seemed to glow.

Hmm, her hair does that wavy thing around her face, and she's got brown eyes; sort of deep and watery, no I mean sparkly, like I could jump in and swim.

A warm feeling bloomed in his chest.

Aargh! No! I've dribbled soup down my front. Thank Emmental the holey cheese, she's not noticed. She's really poised and in control of herself, she'll think I'm a complete dingbat.

'How long have you been at Ellodian?' said Tony, grabbing a napkin.

'Uh, a while.'

'What're you studying?'

'Interesting question,' she said quietly, turning away, 'but not for now.'

Is this an invitation to meet again, or a way of shutting me up?

Her small rosy face gave nothing away. Bobbi kept her brown eyes fixed straight ahead. He went back to his soup remembering the no talking rule.

Was that the reason she'd closed down?

The silence in the hall felt odd, almost spooky. Tony scanned the rows of students dressed in grey gowns, spooning their soup in silence.

This is light years away from the mealtimes at Daisy Bank where shouting, tears, food bombs, plate smashing tournaments and punishment, happened pretty much every day.

'Hi,' said a voice to his left.

'Ignore her,' said Bobbi.

'I'm Vicky.'

A creature, possibly part mole, part human, wearing full school uniform minus crash helmet, sat beside him and offered her tiny hand. Impishly she smiled, revealing a row of yellow pointed teeth. Fine wire-like whiskers swept out from her top lip and fizzled like sparklers.

'Don't touch her, for God's sake,' whispered Bobbi, 'you might catch something.'

'Um, well…' said Tony and made a frown at Bobbi, who flushed an even deeper pink and flicked her hair.

Vicky withdrew her hand and tucked it into her gown. Her small round eyes scrutinised him and he found it hard to look back.

She's so different, so unlike anyone I've met before. Tony swallowed and glanced at her. She's a bit like Gaskin I suppose, but kind of more vulnerable, if that's possible.

'Do you…oh, sorry,' Tony knocked over the salt, 's-sorry, I-I…' With a shaky hand he knocked over the pepper as well and his reddening cheeks began to sting.

What's happening?

Vicky twitched her pointy nose and spoke. 'It's difficult when you first come here to know what to do and how to be,' she said, 'everything's so different and new.'

'Y-yes!' said Tony, leaning forward.

'There isn't a sign to say so, but you can take your crash helmet off at meal times.'

'Aw, thanks!' said Tony, 'but how come most of the students are wearing them while they eat?'

Vicky tipped her tiny head from side to side. 'Some prefer to stay inside the helmet at all times and if you look closely, some have straws.'

The heat from his face cooled. 'I see, thanks very much.' Not caring for the idea of a straw, Tony took off his helmet and changed the subject. 'Can I ask, it might seem odd, but are you mole royalty? If so, have you got an aide? A man called Mr Burr…'

Vicky gathered herself, as if she was about to say something.

'Hold your tongue,' a patrolling tutor snarled.

Bobbi leaned over. 'Did you hear that? She said hold your tongue – that means shut up.'

'Hey!' said Tony, puzzled by Bobbi's sharpness and the fact that there was a tear swelling in her eye, 'there's no law against speaking out.'

Vicky slid down from the bench and scuttled out of the dining room, her bowl of soup untouched.

Bobbi stuffed the remains of her sandwich into her bag, wiped her mouth with a napkin and shook back her long dark hair. 'Well there are laws here,' she said 'and not speaking out is one of them. You've only been here a few weeks, you don't know how this place works.'

'Perhaps you'd better tell me about those laws, and then maybe you could explain the sandwiches?' said Tony.

A voice boomed out from the table at the end of the room.

'Frankly, there appears to be too much talking. I am certain that it is you Bobbi Appledown and you Tony Plumb. Quite frankly, if there is any more talking, you will be sent to Mrs Sherbet's office.'

'See?' said Bobbi from the side of her mouth.

Eight

'The sweats are back McGurney,' said Tony, wiping his hand across the back of his neck.

Sitting on his favourite root, at the bottom of Tony's bed, McGurney nibbled a bit of apple. 'You're quite right Prime Minister.'

Shoving a pillow behind his head, Tony hugged his knees as shadows played on the earthen walls of his bedroom, casting spooky shapes across the floor. At the base of his spine a cold claw pinched, scattering prickly shivers to his toes and finger tips. More sweats. Tony shuddered and huddled up, his eyes tight shut.

Bobbi Appledown's response to Vicky, now that was something sad. Hmm, Vicky had been trying to help and Bobbi had blocked it. Puzzling, odd, malicious even.

The discomfort hung heavily in his chest, limiting breath, but worse than this…

'This is familiar, McGurney, this sense of someone or something good, something special and warm and

nice being blocked or hampered by something bad.'
Tony frowned.

What's that about? I've felt like this before and not just in a little way, in a big way. I know I have, but when?

Queasiness flip-flopped in his stomach like an undigested pancake.

What is this place? Why haven't I got a classroom or somewhere to go? Why can't I speak out? Doesn't anyone want to talk? And what's this bonkers rule about wearing crash helmets? I can't tell who's who, apart from the tutors, who for some reason don't wear them – so it's like everything's secret, like no one's supposed to know who the other really is. Is the world just made up of strangers? Is it all my fault?

Tony gulped. 'I am TOTALLY FREAKED OUT.'
He glanced around his room.

Funny though, it's kind of OK and good that I've got some time to myself, at last. I s'ppose I had tons of time in my bedroom at Mum and Dad's, but that was before the round of so called homes that ended with Daisy Bank, where everybody bothered me, and time alone meant detention or chores or being grounded for days.

The relief slid away.

Come to think of it though, being in my bedroom at Mum and Dad's wasn't really me time either, more like pure, bottom-of-the-bucket loneliness.

'OK…' Tony snorted and clenched his fist. 'So now I'm in the world with time to myself, McGurney, and what've I got? As if Bobbi, Vicky and Ellodian aren't enough, I've got this letter and these questions.' He slapped the letter down on his quilt.

McGurney fixed him with a beady eye and fluttered down from his perch. 'Pull yer socks up!' he said, clawing his way up the bed to Tony's side.

'Something's definitely wrong,' Tony whispered. The image of the woman with beetle eyes floated into his mind.

'Ask no questions hear no lies…'

The panic returned like a swift punch and his heart began to bang. 'McGurney, I feel awful. Does this worrying, spooky feeling come from inside, like from history and memories and stuff, or is it about now, being here at Ellodian?' Tony sighed, 'I suppose it could be both, but whatever it is, I need to start thinking normal thoughts.'

McGurney cocked his head.

'Thinking sometimes hurts me, McGurney.'

'Right,' said McGurney, 'it's time you and I had a frank discussion.' Tony's head shot up and he stared at the parrot. 'Oh, spare me the theatricals, will you? My vocabulary is extensive, I went to Harvard and I studied there well before you were born.'

'Wow…you can…'

'Yes, I can. We'll get to know each other better, but not now. Right now, we need to work things out, but first you need a wake-up call. Have you any idea where you are or why you are here?'

'Er…the questions in the letter?'

'Yes, that as well. Look, a boy nearly died that time you were in the river. Good job you rescued him, but stay alert, will you? Did it not strike you as odd that Mrs Sherbet didn't help, call an ambulance or even suggest you took Gaskin to the sick bay? Did it not concern you that Prospect didn't question her actions?'

Tony hung his head. *It's true, this does worry me, it's just that…*

A thought chariot clattered by.

'*…Ask no questions, hear no lies…*'

Catching McGurney's unblinking, beady stare, Tony managed to derail the thought chariot and as it skidded to a halt, he lowered his eyes.

'This is making my brain hurt, but I guess what you're saying is that I'm switched off, not paying attention,' said Tony, taking a deep breath. 'You want me to start thinking, don't you?'

McGurney jumped from the bed back to his favourite root; his eye, side on, remained fixed and beadier than ever.

Tony sat up straight. 'I guess there's a lot happening here at Ellodian that I'm not questioning, and a lot of stuff in this letter too.' Tony read the letter again. 'Masses, like all my life's problems. D'you know, I think there's loads my parents didn't tell me.'

'That is correct,' said McGurney. 'I'm encouraged to see that you have decided to start thinking. A process has begun.'

Process? Sounds a bit like social services speak.

Just then, a question bounced out of a passing thought chariot; a question that had circled his mental arena many times.

'What do you think I should do, I mean, for the best?' Tony's voice sounded different, it was sharper, clearer. 'Tell me, McGurney.'

'Well you know that you are held here, largely by your own needs, and there is no escape from this place. Not at present. You are here for a reason and that letter is a guide.'

A sudden lightness exploded in his chest. McGurney's words had pushed an obstacle away and instantly, questions were everywhere, questions that really, really needed answering.

'So, I'm here for a reason? To find out about Mum and Dad and what happened, to them and to me. That might be useful, helpful even. Cool, but…couldn't I just leave and maybe do it later?'

'Run away you mean?' said McGurney.

The thought chariots set off, whizzing around, but this time with an energy he could harness, an energy that could be useful, and most important, his mind was alive with a power he didn't feel afraid of. In less than a tick of time a whole new space in his head opened up, as if doors once jammed were being flung open, one after the other. Bang, bang, bang and a clear-cut brightness, like lightning, caught Tony in a sharp electric flash.

'It's true, Mum and Dad were in a very bad place. I remember Dad falling about, incapable. Sometimes he couldn't even stand up and was flat out on the sofa for days.' He swung his legs off the bed. 'Y'know once, I was taking a bath, and Dad came in and started taking these little 'secret packages,' he called them, from behind a loose tile, and saying, "keep things quiet, Tony, don't tell, don't grass, not even to your friends." Well, that wasn't difficult, I didn't have any friends.'

McGurney tipped his head to one side.

'Dad did crazy, crazy things, like pulling Mum outside, at dawn, to help make a bonfire and cook frozen pizza. The next day all the grass was scorched, cats were everywhere eating leftovers, and all the cardboard wrappers blew out into the street.'

Tony closed his eyes.

He could see his parents vividly; always clinking glasses and egging each other on. Cheery by mid-afternoon, bad tempered by tea-time and fighting and shouting through the nine o'clock news. Then they'd collapse on the sofa, zoned out and zombified until the following afternoon, when the whole horrible cycle would begin again. Tony remembered the pungent smell that forever hung around the house, those sick making, hot, spicy notes that made his eyes sting and his nose run. Detestable. He pictured the empty cupboards and mouldy fridges, remembering how he'd been so hungry, he'd once stolen a bag of crisps from the local shop. He still felt bad about that. Back home – beer cans were everywhere; wine bottles lay strewn across the floor and the neighbours' lights were flicking on. Then the police would knock, no, bang on the door; Mum would cry, and Dad would shout, and Dad would be taken in for questioning.

Lost in his memories, Tony stared into the middle distance, thinking more about life before he lost Mum and Dad.

A light breeze blew in from the hole in the ceiling, jolting him from the reverie.

How long has everything been clogged up by these dreadful memories from the past?

Drawing a breath, he cast a glance at McGurney who stayed calm, silent and ever watchful.

'Tony, there's something else you need to know.'

Tony's eyes rounded large and wide, his limbs suddenly limp and his throat tight.

McGurney ruffled his feathers. 'I cannot stay with you. You must go ahead alone.'

'What!' Tears sprang quickly. 'Wh-wh-where are you going?'

'Back to the Congo, my wife's been having trouble with our teenager, but I will come back Tony, when I can.'

'Y-you have a wife, a-a – and – and a family?'

'Yes, Tony, I do.'

A hard ball of something he couldn't swallow, rose up in his throat.

'I'm not good at goodbyes,' said the parrot testing his wings, 'but what I will say to you is this. I wouldn't leave you, if I didn't think you could manage. Work out those questions and in addition, Tony, question Ellodian.'

'Er – what…?'

'So now I wish you well. Good luck and goodbye.'

McGurney flapped his sleek grey wings, swept up through the window and out to the snowy, grey sky.

Tony's pillow took a heavy punch.

Hope of answering any of those questions is now impossible. All those ideas about my parents, all that clear thinking, all that urgency… It's all gone, it's left me… Gone like McGurney, gone like my mum and dad.

Punch, punch, punch.

The snow drifting in from the skylight, began to melt on the floor.

Burying his face in his pillow, he let out a deep blubbering sob.

The wounds in his mind screamed out for comfort; their rawness quickly covered with layers and layers of soft cotton wool. The part of Tony that had seen and understood things from the past in three-dimensional clarity and framed in a bright white light, now returned to darkened slumber.

Somewhere though, hidden deep in the mind of Tony Plumb, an important process was well under way.

Nine

He needed some air.

'I haven't got a timetable, so bunking off isn't really bunking off – no lessons to bunk off from. Coolio.'

Bouncing twice on his bed, he shot up high enough to grip the dead ferns that clustered, like a rusty necklace, around the skylight. Within seconds he hauled himself out onto the cool damp earth of the world outside. The sharp air of late autumn crept inside his crash helmet and tickled his nostrils. It was snowing lightly and as the afternoon shifted into evening, the ground took on a violet hue as if lit by fluorescent tubes.

On his right was a copse. He could make out some students stumbling around in their gowns and crash helmets, the yellowness of their headgear bright against the dark background of the wood.

Funny, students didn't usually do much in a group, apart from eat or go to assembly, so what's this little bunch up to? I haven't seen those tall pointy trees before and this wood's new, I don't recognise it. Where's the House of Miniature Mailboats?

A fair-haired boy passed between the trees; a boy without a crash helmet.

A second later, Tony glimpsed the figure again. He wore a blue jumper and jeans. Spinning around, Tony raked the wood with his eyes.

He's gone.

All grew still and silent. A single bird flew up and out through the canopy.

What's that?

Muffled sounds like voices drifted between the trees.

Someone's speaking – must be a member of staff. I can deffo hear voices, someone's chattering, but there's no one there.

Then a laugh rang out through the wood.

Hang on, there he is again; the boy, moving between two trees…Now where's he gone? It's like the tree trunks are an opening, like a gate, and the boy's just walked past. Wait a minute – I recognise him!

A wheel fell off a parked thought chariot, and Tony's inquisitiveness swelled.

Running towards the trees, he skidded to a stop. The noise of traffic pounded as if he were on a busy street. A car hooted, doors slammed, and someone shouted.

'Taxi!'

Tony held his head. The thought chariots had now galvanised and started to spin everywhere, colliding,

67

screeching and bouncing off the walls of his mind. Colours and shapes whizzed by, funny smells and weird voices bubbled up like someone gargling. A crack, as if someone had broken through a door, exploded from behind and turning his head, Tony locked eyes with the blue-eyed boy; the boy from the bus stop.

Whooaa! It's him and this is familiar. It's Evensham, I'm in Evensham.

In an effort to stop his hands trembling, Tony shoved them under his knees.

How come I'm sitting on a bench? I can't stop my knees from knocking, I'm sweating, I'm outside the Pick'n'Mix, my mouth's as dry as ch-chalk. What's happening?

The blue-eyed boy said something about Daisy Bank.

'…Anyhow, I left ages ago and now I'm starting at a new place…'

Tony slowly took in the features of the other boy and tried to focus. 'Ellodian, are you going to Ellodian? Were you in the wood?' said Tony.

''Ello what? What're you on about? Nah, I'm going to Midway House, I might do a course.'

Tony studied his face.

'Whatcha lookin' at? Stop starin' at me. Freako. You were always nuts, you know that don't you?' said the blue-eyed boy.

Tony reached up and touched his head. No crash helmet. Was Sherbet around? Where's Ellodian?

'Wanna play some pool?' asked the boy. 'I know a place where they'll serve under-agers. Wanna try some Rushpop?' he waved a brightly coloured can. 'C'mon.' The boy got up and started to cross the road.

Tony's clothes were damp from sweat and streaked with mud. Was that mud from Ellodian? He scratched his head.

Blue-eyes called him from across the street, his voice carried by a strong breeze. A piece of paper fluttered by and stuck to the side of Tony's shoe. It had some writing on it. He bent down.

It's someone's shopping list. Coleslaw, watercress, soda water, bubble bath, shower cap, ice cream.

Tony's memory jerked into action.

'Wait!' Tony leapt after the blue-eyed boy, narrowly missing the number seven bus, 'I need to ask you about the waterfall.'

The blond head darted amongst the market stalls, before the boy emerged on the pavement.

'C'mon, c'mon, over here!' The boy beckoned before turning and running down an alley.

His heart thumping, Tony followed, catching up with him in a loading yard, surrounded by railings. Blue-eyes stood in front of two big metal doors.

'It's in here.'

I'm not going in there, no way. They're likely the doors to hell – PRYVAT – weird spelling and painted in red. Huh! and what's that dangling padlock?

'Got any money?' said the boy.

'N-no, I'm sorry, listen I need to ask you something.'

'It'll cost yer.' The boy smirked and prodded Tony in the chest.

'I haven't got any money, it's about what you said about my parents...'

'No money, no answers, nutcase.' The boy grabbed some railings and swung himself up onto a small wall.

'Please, I need to know more about my mum and dad. You said something about them jumping off a waterfall...'

'They did, everybody at Daisy Bank knows that and more. Gimme your watch.'

'Please, just tell me what you know.'

The boy looped his arms around the railings and pulling up his legs, planted his feet in Tony's chest and pushed hard. Tony fell on the cobbled yard and a sharp pain shot up his back. The boy pounced and circling Tony's neck with his hands, began to squeeze. Tony brought up his knees, flung Blue-eyes off, scrambled to his feet and pinned the boy's arms to his sides.

'Tell me... Ouch!' Tony let go to hold his throbbing shin, and in seconds his hand was warm, sticky and wet. 'I'm bleeding.'

'I'm bleeeeee–ding.' The boy laughed and ran off, back onto the street.

Tony limped out of the alley and found the nearest bench. Drawing his knee up, he tried to stem the blood with his sleeve as he scanned the busy street for the blue-eyed boy.

He's gone, but he said something, he said everybody knew about Mum and Dad. So, there must be others from Daisy Bank who could tell me. Let me think, there was Pele and Anita, but they left and went abroad. Someone called Robbie and a girl who nobody liked called Dilly or was it Lily? This is useless. Wait a minute, why do I need to go on a youngster hunt for other Daisy Bank inmates, when Bendy Leggett will know? I bet she's known what happened all along.

People milled around the shops, their shapes a colourful, muddled fuzz.

All I want is the truth, I want the truth.

'I'm thirteen,' he said out loud. Shoppers eyed him and hurried on. 'I'm thirteen and I have a right to know. I have a right to know. Hey,' he said to no-one in particular, 'wouldn't you want to know if someone said your parents had jumped off a waterfall? Wouldn't you want to know why?'

A small space opened up around him.

'Why, did my parents jump off a waterfall and leave me alone to go into care?'

'Can I help?'

Tony looked at the young woman who'd materialised by his side. She wore a blue and white uniform and a badge that said 'Jenning's Chemist' and 'Jeanie' in felt tip pen underneath.

'Yes please, Jeanie. Could you point me in the direction of social services?'

Ten

'Tony Plumb?'

Tony pushed himself up from the bench...*Hang on, no bench, this is a damp floor, a corridor floor.* Holly sprouted from the wall beside him and something furry just whizzed down a hole. What happened to Jeanie?

'Is that you Jeanie?'

The school elder bustled up.

'No, I am not a genie. It's Plumb, isn't it? I thought so. Frankly you are setting a bad example, sitting on the floor indeed, and frankly, I think you should return to your classroom promptly.'

Deffo a complete waste of time telling her about classroom deprivation. Wait though, she might be able to help me.

'I'm looking for a chemist, I mean, no, actually I'm looking for Bendy, Ms Leggett. She's got dark curly hair, she's not a chemist, she's a...'

Tony glanced at Miss Frankly's face as it loomed up close, suddenly interested.

Aaarrgh! Wrong! I'm walking into a trap. Reverse! Reverse!

'Who?' said Miss Frankly.

'Er, no one.'

'You've legged it from where? Who are you looking for?'

'Nowhere. No one.'

'Frankly that's a bit odd. You just said you were looking for a chemist and a girl or a woman. What are you up to Plumb?'

'N-n-nothing.'

'Tell me her name and I'll help you.'

Tony shrank back. That sounded a bit too much like '…trust me, I won't hurt you…'

'Don't know.'

'What do you mean by a chemist, Plumb? Is this about drugs?'

Tony shook his head.

'Well then, tell me her name.'

Tony began to squirm.

'I said NAME.'

'B – B – Ben,' said Tony, feeling hot and then hotter. His visor started to steam up.

'Ben? I thought you said the person was female?' Miss Frankly peered at him over her spectacles.

'There are lots of odd things here aren't there?'

'Don't change the subject, Plumb.'

Tony began to edge his way along the corridor. Miss Frankly followed.

'Ben – are you sure that's her name? Frankly, I don't believe we currently have a Ben on our books. Are you fibbing, Plumb?'

Why all this sudden interest in what he said? Tutors, in fact pretty much everyone he'd met so far at Ellodian, apart from Vicky, had been distant and even dismissive.

Miss Frankly's face came closer.

And closer…

Even through his helmet, her breath smelled of herbal tea and droplets of moisture hung visibly from the hairs on her chin.

Oh no! She's going to open her mouth…that's too creepy.

'My parrot told me I should be more sociable, so I figured I'd make friends with a girl called Benzo, er no, Benny-Lynn, but I don't know where to find her.'

'Benzo you say?' Miss Frankly's eyes darted left, then right.

'Er, no, Benaline, no I meant Benny-Lynn. Her name's Benny-Lynn.'

Breathe, breathe, breathe.

Miss Frankly's eyes narrowed to slits.

'Frankly, I suggest you forget about all this nonsense and get a grip, you are speaking gibberish. Frankly, I suspect you are an isolate and quite mad, yes, unhinged, seeking so-called friends that aren't

74

there. Benzo, Ben, Benny-Lyn, Benaline and talk of a chemist. Very suspicious indeed and furthermore, talking to genies and believing a parrot can advise you. Frankly nonsense! Report to sick bay tomorrow, after assembly.'

And with that she'd gone.

Stumbling along the damp, fern cluttered corridor a few minutes later, Miss Frankly's voice drifted back into earshot. He slowed down.

This must be her office.

He pressed his ear to the door; she was speaking to someone on the phone. Straining and trying not to breathe too loudly, he could just about make out what she was saying.

'Frankly, Mrs Sherbet, I think he's onto something.'

Tony stiffened.

'Frankly yes…what to do…yes, yes, I see…'

A long paused settled.

Has she put the phone down? Is she going to fling open the door and drag me in?

Tony stood very still, his breath visible in the coldness.

'Yes.' Miss Frankly's voice fell to a whisper, but Tony could just about hear what she said.

'Yes, I'll get Heapey on to him.'

Eleven

Jessica Heapey
Registered Psychotherapist
Please ring the bell

Pulling on the jangly bell at the pre-arranged hour he wished, as he always did, that he'd washed his hair or at least cleaned his teeth. He waited. He knocked again. Eventually she came and stood aside to let him in. Mrs Heapey was small, round and had turquoise eyes. Did she seem a little less calm than the last time? Even though they'd met every week for a while, Mrs Heapey never talked about herself.

Still, I know her a bit. She's sort of, well she's like, um, she's always…Hmm, actually, it's a bit difficult to work out anything about her at all; how she's feeling or what she thinks. The only thing I can work out is that I think she's nice.

Tugging the wrinkles out of his jumper, Tony studied her eyes but all he could see was a kindly twinkle. Sitting down in his usual chair and putting his crash helmet by his feet, he waited for Mrs Heapey to settle and the session to begin.

'You know that list of questions I got from Mrs Sherbet? Well I've made a bit of progress, I mean, I've made some friends, well one friend so far, he's a mole and I might make more mole friends.'

Mrs Heapey sat back in her chair. 'It's true that friends can help us find out things about ourselves, but Tony, tell me what you think the moles are for?'

'They're cute, but I think they're used as cheap labour,' he said, 'here to dig out extensions and build new rooms.' His gaze slipped sideways, and he leaned forward. 'To be honest, I think the cook here also puts them in the soup.'

Mrs Heapey's face remained kindly, open and inquiring.

'So, we might be eating the moles?'

'Well I haven't ever seen you in the dining hall, Mrs Heapey, so I wouldn't know if you were eating the soup, but I do know someone who doesn't eat it. Bobbi Appledown doesn't eat the soup; she gets sandwiches from a takeaway, wherever that might be.'

Mrs Heapey nodded. 'I like the idea that the moles might be inside us, the products of their labour being digested as we speak.' A small smile played about her lips.

'A mole inside me? Cool idea. I think I know what you mean. Changing the sub, there's one thing I didn't say last time and it's something I think you should know.' He looked at his shoes. 'It's about my mum and dad. I don't think my mum was as hooked as my dad was.'

Mrs Heapey raised an eyebrow.

'I mean she deffo did drugs, but I think she just did it to help him out.'

'Help him out?'

'Mmm, you know, I think she was just trying to show some kind of support and...maybe...things got out of hand, or something like that...do you know what I mean?'

'I'm not sure that I do. It doesn't sound like a helpful arrangement, could you say a bit more?'

'Well, I'll try.' He cleared his throat.

'I think it was more that, maybe, he made her bad.'

'Do you think that it was all your father's fault?'

Tony closed his eyes. A silence descended.

Mrs Heapey's face remained calm, constant and inquiring.

'I didn't really know all this when they died, I was only five, but I had some ideas and social workers filled me in with bits y'know, but I think it's right that my dad made her behave badly. I don't think she would've done anything wrong, maybe not even at all...if it wasn't for him.

'What do you remember about your parents?'

'Well Mum was lovely, sort of nice and kind. She used to make me sandwiches and put them in a little container, so I could take them with me when I went out to play. I really liked that. I thought she did her best. Having these sandwiches in that little box made me feel like I was a special person…Do you see?'

Mrs Heapey tilted her head. 'Sandwiches like Bobbi Appledown's?'

'My mum and dad died and, and, it might have been… their fault, their decision to go. The boy I met at the bus stop said they jumped. But I don't think my mum would have jumped if it wasn't for my dad.' His eyes misted over, and he took a hankie from Mrs Heapey's tissue box. 'I think Mum wanted to stay with me…I think…I think…'

'What do you think, Tony?'

'I think my mum might have…well…I think she probably…no, definitely liked me a lot more than she liked my dad.' Tony sneaked a glimpse at her to check out what she might be thinking, but as usual Mrs Heapey gave nothing away.

'I don't want to seem like, big headed or anything, it's just that she used to chat to me in a really nice way and then when he came into the room, she'd stop, and she'd have to make a fuss of him.'

'Have to…?'

'Yes, y'know, in case he got jealous.'

'Jealous?'

'Well, jealous of the thing we had, me and Mum; our special relationship.'

'I see,' said Mrs Heapey.

'I think she loved me a lot. I think she cared for me tons more than my dad did and I cared for her more than he ever could. He just wasn't bothered.'

'You were five years old when you lost your parents,' said Mrs Heapey quietly.

Tony's eyes found the turquoise gems.

Mrs Heapey continued. 'It's just that you seem to remember quite a bit about how good your mum was and your dad, in comparison, seems to be a demon. Do you think you might have wanted him to go or disappear so you could be with your mum – just you two?'

The silence that followed sucked Tony to its depths. Clattering by, the thought chariots carried boxes labelled: 'parents only', 'three's a crowd', 'gooseberry' and 'not in front of the child'. A familiar tightness gathered in his throat.

'I really loved my mum.'

Mrs Heapey nodded. 'Yes, you did and still do. You have a lot of love within you Tony.' It was time for the session to end.

'I'll see you next week,' she said, holding open the door.

As he stepped out of Mrs Heapey's room, a funny smell crept into his helmet and a thump, thump, thump noise drifted into earshot, getting louder every second. Tony glanced down the corridor to a curve in the passageway where the increasing sound echoed off the walls.

Whoever, or whatever it is, is about to come into view.

Leaping behind a curtain of ivy, Tony spied a plump boy, about his own age and without a crash helmet, approaching Mrs Heapey's room. Without knocking, he entered quickly, slamming the door behind him. A great waft of throat-strangling stinkiness engulfed Tony's hideout.

This must be another patient. Odd, he didn't seem to be wearing many clothes, and that smell. Rotting fish and bad eggs.

'Good evening Perfax,' Tony heard Mrs Heapey say. Her voice seemed calm on the surface as if everything was normal, but underneath rang a disturbing note, tight, chilly and crackling with terror.

Twelve

Tony rubbed his belly. 'It must be lunchtime soon.'

The food at Ellodian was beginning to be a bit of a problem since he'd spoken to Mrs Heapey about the possibility of the brown soup containing moles. Their last conversation had been a bit odd. The idea of having a mole inside him, an internal mole, what a bonkers idea! Tony chuckled but shivered at the same time.

A memory tippled out of a wobbly chariot, and he sat up quickly. When he was very young, his dad had taken him to the pictures. They'd gone to see a film about a man who was smuggling top-secret information out of a country that was at war. The film, Dad said, was about espionage and that meant spies. Stories about special agents or undercover cops were Dad's favourite. Tony remembered watching the film because his dad seemed calm and relaxed.

'Why's that man giving away the other man's secrets?'

Tony had asked. His dad leaned forward, shrouding his son in a cloak of boozy fumes.

'He's a mole, an informant, a grass, he's a spy and he tells the other side what our hero is up to. He passes on the secrets. Now shut up will yer and let me watch this film.'

Tony sat in silence and tried to concentrate on the film. There was a lot he hadn't understood, but he did understand that a mole was another name for a spy who spilled secrets.

He remembered walking home.

His dad had said something like, 'You know Son, it's better not to tell anybody anything, that way they don't have anything on you. Better to keep the family's secrets, secret. Do yer get my meaning?'

Tony said he did, and after that he never talked to anyone much about anything and always kept an eye out for a possible spy.

When his parents died it'd felt a bit awkward when coroners and people in the courts, like social workers and psychologists, had asked stuff about his parents and their habits, and not wanting to grass, he'd mostly said he didn't know.

Hmm, the moles in the soup, the moles I've swallowed, and the moles that might now be inside of me. What if the moles inside of me know my secrets; secrets about me?

A thought clattered into his available mind. Informing moles, internal moles, moles who could be undercover spies.

What if an internal mole is digging in my mind right now? A mole capable of telling tales on what it found there? What if thoughts and ideas that I've hidden away are being dug up by my internal mole, only to be exposed when the mole thinks the moment is right? Could there be a mole inside of me capable of spilling secrets that I'm not yet ready to hear? Secrets I've been keeping from myself?

Thirteen

Tony knocked on the door of Mrs Heapey's room.

'Come in,' said a bright voice, and he entered.

It had been only a week since his last appointment, but a week was beginning to feel like quite a long time.

In truth Tony you have missed Mrs Heapey — and the sight of her welcoming smile and kind turquoise eyes are lifting your heart more than you anticipated.

Thank you, Mole.

Tony silently acknowledged the work of his internal spy.

I wonder if a therapy session is the best place to take such a busy, emotional informant? Especially one with this level of nosiness and potential to blurt stuff out? What if I'm not ready to deal with it?

He pushed his hands into his pocket to make sure that the Christmas card he'd made for Mrs Heapey was still there. He followed her to their usual chairs and they sat down. The room seemed familiar, solid and comfortable.

'I've been doing some thinking.'

'Aah,' said Mrs Heapey, which made Tony chuckle.

'Yes, my thinking is coming along. It's about the moles in the soup, y'see…'

'The moles?'

'Yes, I've got this idea about an inside mole excavator. A mole operating inside of me, like a spy, an informant, passing messages between the bits of my mind that I know about and the bits I don't; and maybe don't want to. I think some bits are wrapped up in cotton wool and those, I reckon, are the bits I'm trying to avoid knowing about, if you see what I mean.'

'Yes, Tony I think I do. We all need to keep some things hidden from our everyday, wakeful, awareness,' said Mrs Heapey thoughtfully.

'Mmm,' said Tony, sensing she knew what he meant.

'One thing I do know is that my dad was bad, and I don't ever want to be like him.'

'Hmm I see,' said Mrs Heapey. 'Has there ever been a male in your life that you have respected?'

He knitted his brows. 'McGurney, my parrot.'

'I thought for a moment you said, McGurney my parent.'

Hesitating for a second, Tony smiled. 'Well he's much better at looking after me than my dad was,' he said, laughing.

You might well laugh, but don't you think it's quite sad that a boy like yourself only has a parrot as an adult figure; someone to look up to as a role model? You're angry about how your dad was Tony, you know you are and you should speak to Mrs Heapey about how you are feeling.

He swallowed hard.

'Yes Tony, what is it?' said Mrs Heapey.

'I'm angry with my dad. He was a no good, useless, silly idiot. He wasn't interested in anything I did. F'rinstance, I liked paddling in the water and stuff, I used to go down to a stream near my house, well it was pretty wide in parts like a river, but Dad never came. He was just too interested in himself.' Tony clenched his fist. 'Y'know I'm really, really angry with him. He was such a nincompoop, out of it, shouting and throwing things. He broke the cupboard doors in the kitchen. What a waste of time…'

…and Mum is lovely and innocent…and good…

'My mum was too good for him. I mean, I think she should have taken me away with her. We could have run off together, and then everything would've been great…do y'see…?'

'Tony, you told me last time that your mother took drugs.'

Tony stared.

'I didn't.'

'You did.'

He frowned at her.

You did…aaarrgh!

The bit of Tony's mind that he could control just squished the internal mole.

'I don't remember saying that my mum did that. Well I s'ppose, it's possible that she could have done... But come to think about it, I doubt it really. It was my dad who took stuff, no question. Hey, before I forget, Mrs Sherbet's invited me to tea!'

Did a spiky-edged cloud just skim across Mrs Heapey's face?

You just changed the subject pretty quickly there Tony, and yes, a cloud did just skim across Mrs Heapey's face. You know full well that your mum took...aaarrgh!

'It should be fun,' said Tony, his voice rising. Sherbet met me on a corridor and just asked me. I hope we have something cool to eat, y'know like scones. Scones are ace, especially with strawberry jam. It's up there, written on my calendar, can't wait.'

Rubbish. You're bluffing to get yourself out of this awkward situation and if you're not careful you'll become overexcited and giddy and feel stupid later. Now you know this, you might ignore it, but you have the choice...

He felt Mrs Heapey's eyes upon him.

'I guess we can't un-remember, but we can forget. I think at this point in time, I'm remembering what you said; that your mum took drugs. This is something that is both sad and bad for her, and for you, and something that currently you have forgotten because you want your mum to be good and special. Perhaps the internal mole has hidden this memory deeper than other stuff, so you don't remember, and you don't think it's true. My sense is that your memory is good, and that in time

88

you will remember.' The twinkle in her turquoise eyes was back.

He looked carefully at the small, round woman sitting opposite.

Things just shifted. What she's just said's pushed me on into a new situation. Mrs Heapey's caught something, like gold in a sieve. The gold might have tumbled free, but Mrs Heapey saw it, caught hold of it, and remembered.

'…We can't un-remember…'

Tony wriggled in his chair and glanced at his shoes. 'My dad took me to the pictures once. We saw a spy film. I s'ppose he can't have been that bad if he took me to see a film, and the zoo; we once went to the zoo.'

'Mmm. Did your mum come along?'

'No, she didn't like spy films or animals. I think she would have been at home.'

Probably in bed, zonked out. Sometimes you never saw her until mid-afternoon. Once she set alight to the quilt didn't she…?

Tears gathered beneath the ginger fringe. Mrs Heapey leaned forward a little.

'Perhaps we'll talk about your mum a bit more next time?' she said.

He nodded.

'All this is helping, isn't it? I mean it will help me, won't it, with Mrs Sherbet's letter?'

'Do you mean – will finding out more about your early family life help with the questions?'

'Yes, that.'

'I think what you're trying to do is break through some thoughts and feelings that have so far masked a truth and blocked you from understanding something important.'

'Like what?'

Tony's question was answered with a small smile. It was time to go. Mrs Heapey stood up and turned to the door. Tony followed.

A glint of something…caught his eye…

What's that? A brandy bottle shoved behind a plant pot! Is Mrs Heapey drinking brandy? Does she drink brandy in the morning?

His mind at once plunged into a thick fog. Inhaling quickly, he drew in the scent of Mrs Heapey and her room. Ripe, fruity notes tickled his nose, pungent and smoky.

It smells like, like them…

A dagger of ice sliced quickly through his heart and he left swiftly, the Christmas card still in his pocket.

Fourteen

It was Christmas Day. His stomach rumbled.

But will there be anything other than brown soup and bread? Daisy Bank at least got fried chicken from the takeaway. True, it was the scrapings from Christmas Eve, chewy, gristly, buried in cold batter and eaten in a corridor, but still.

He scanned the rows of student diners.

You're looking out for Bobbi?

Only to wish her a Merry Christmas, Mole.

You mean you really want to kiss her?

A slow burn crept up his face. He scanned the room hoping to see her, but also to check if anyone was acting as if privy to the voice of his internal mole.

Waving a Christmas napkin folded carefully into the shape of a swan, Gaskin caught his eye, and grinned.

'Hey, Gaskin that napkin's pretty cool.'

Nodding, Gaskin said nothing about moles, but licked his soup spoon and quietly took a few more napkins from Cook's trolley. Mrs Basher, the cook, didn't notice.

The paper swan had an arched neck and pointy wings opening out from its red, green and gold body. The swan had the words '*sMash Crime*' written on the curve of its neck which, when the napkin was unfolded, revealed the greeting 'Merry Christmas'.

'Look at that,' said Tony, and both giggled. Gaskin began to make more swans.

Tony nudged Gaskin and pointed to another row of tables. 'People have been very busy; red crepe paper party hats – flippin' heck!' More giggling. Tony darted a glance at the tutors sitting at their usual elevated table at the front of the hall, 'and what's more, no one seems to mind us talking – a-ma-zing.'

Tony began to feel almost jolly.

Mrs Sherbet arrived with Prospect trailing behind her. The headmistress wore a voluminous dress of acid yellow velvet, which clashed spectacularly with her crimson hair. Hung about her neck was an opal the size of a gull's egg, sinking at least an inch into the thick fleshiness of her throat. Mrs Sherbet glided to her seat, as a steamer into port.

'She's actually smiling,' said Tony, 'that's good to see and makes a change.'

Prospect appeared much the same as usual, shuffling along, tired and grey; a bowl of brown soup in his hand.

There's Bobbi. Get that silver dress beneath her gown, and her hair's all shimmery, like something polished.

Hmm, maybe it's the candlelight. What's that stuff on her mouth? It's lipstick, a sort of shiny lemon colour, or is it orange? Hard to tell, but it looks sticky.

Beside Bobbi stood Miss Woosey the librarian, serving herself some soup. Miss Woosey leaned in towards Bobbi.

Quick, they're whispering, get close.

'Won't be a mo, Gaskin.'

'Merry Christmas, Bobbi,' Miss Woosey was saying, 'I love your apricot lip gloss.'

Bobbi's face brightened as Miss Woosey moved away towards the staff table. Tony stood back and watched as Bobbi removed the damp oak leaf Miss Woosey had unintentionally transferred to the front of her dress.

Tony returned to his seat beside Gaskin.

If I'm going to get closer to her this Christmas, then I'd better know exactly what I'm dealing with. I've now got complete confirmation; this is not Lemon Lipstick but is in fact Apricot Lip Gloss.

'Soup?' said Gaskin. Tony held out his bowl.

Eating this soup might encourage my internal mole in its task to tell tales on my unknown mind. Sounds a bit risky but I might make a discovery, find out something about me.

Like you're sweet on Bobbi.

Not true, Mole. Well, maybe it is.

'This soup's not bad,' he said. Gaskin nodded, tucking into some grapes.

Bobbi came to sit at his table, but four places down in a seat that was free. They exchanged smiles and

Tony's heart hopped. Bobbi made a little movement with her fingers like she was playing a silent trumpet.

In the scheme of things, this might be the best Christmas ever.

Oooh! la! la!

Cut it out, Mole.

Mrs Sherbet made a tinging noise with a spoon on her glass.

'Our talented librarian Miss Woosey will now delight us with a little recitation penned by herself entitled…' Mrs Sherbet leaned over to Miss Frankly. 'What's it called again?'

Miss Frankly whispered something.

'…entitled "Frankly When Pansies Thrive and Lungwort Frankly Bursts in Eagerness for Spring". Thank you, Miss Woosey.'

Soft clapping fluttered around the hall.

Miss Woosey stood; put a second pair of spectacles over the pair she was already wearing and cleared her throat.

'And as it was with monstrous, darkened lardy clouds
Like plumpy lumps of treacle sponge
Burnt sharp in baking
The sunshine stabbed the land with rays and
Light, behold, without a plug, dazzled and
With this blast of zapparoo we saw
The pansies thrive and lungwort burst,
In eagerness for spring.

Oh spring! Thou art so perky,
Perk, perk, perky,
Giving winter the big heave ho!
No pleasure in those biting months
That kept our noses drip, drip dripping
And our toes like frozen sausages
With no chips to keep them warm, or beans
Our eyes under bobble hats await to see
The pansies thrive and lungwort burst
In eagerness for spring.'

'Very good, Miss Woosey, I'm sure we'll all flock to the library after lunch to hear you read that again.'

Clapping hard, Tony caught a glimpse of a student, likely a boy from the looks of it, rushing past. Scampering in circles, the late-comer pulled at his crash helmet and tried to find a seat.

Ker-rip, ker-runch! The student's gown caught on the very same bolt that had felled Tony a few months before. Falling at speed, the student skidded across the floor coming to a halt between Tony and Gaskin.

'Oh no! Not again!' Tony sprang to help.

'Gaskin, free his gown. Hi, I'm Tony, are you OK?' Tony eased off the helmet.

'Th-thanks,' said the boy, 'I'm Nelson, aaoww!'

'You've gashed your face. Careful now. Hang on.'

Grabbing a handful of swans, Tony tried to stem the flow of blood. Everyone had witnessed the fall and a hush descended. All eyes flew to Mrs Sherbet.

'Typical, she hasn't even noticed what's happened, she's hopeless,' said Tony applying more swans. 'Look at her, devouring a full pineapple, completely oblivious.'

Gaskin squeaked.

Smack, guzzle, slurp, dribble, Mrs Sherbet continued with her lunch.

Mrs Sherbet's deffo in the wrong job. Now Prospect's started to wave, he thinks people are looking at them to be friendly.

The elders sat and stared straight ahead, like a row of Easter Island statues.

'Could someone pass the ginger?' said Mrs Sherbet.

Tony bent down and helped Nelson onto the bench.

Miss Frankly rattled a teaspoon against her glass. The hall shifted its stare from the headmistress to Miss Frankly.

'Frankly', she said, 'I find it simply reassuring that after all my years at Ellodian, we have NOT bowed to the modernisers who have wanted us to remove the yellow helmet from Ellodian's uniform.' The dining hall remained silent. Davinia Frankly continued.

'Frankly,' she said, 'This instance that we have all just had the misfortune to witness, proves the necessity for the yellow helmet, irrefutably and without doubt. Frankly…'

'Thank you, Miss Frankly,' said Mrs Sherbet without so much as a glance up from her pineapple, but this time the diners didn't resume their eating.

'HELL'S CURSES ON YOU! You useless, pathetic twit!' blasted Tony and threw Nelson's crash helmet across the dining hall floor, where it bounced and doinged off jutting rocks and knobbly roots, narrowly missing a small student.

Yes! We have contact with our anger! Er – Careful Tony.

Mrs Sherbet dropped her pineapple and looked up. One or two students gasped, one or two began a slow ripple of applause and one or two climbed under the tables to hide.

Tony's chest heaved quickly in and out.

What? No! I hadn't reckoned Mole would spew out THAT! – What have I said? – stuff I hadn't meant to say. No way! Even worse, now I've blurted, I can't take it back. Thanks a lot, Mole.

Just doing my job...

Tears slipped.

I've repeated what Dad said to Mum – this is bad, very bad. He yelled this at Mum when he was being horrible. No, no, no!

His face became red and raw as tears spurted and his nose got sticky and wet. Anguish bit deep into his trembling heart and he completely tuned out of his surroundings.

The students, the staff and all the people in the hall, including Rownbout, the gardener who had arrived with a leylandii in a tub, just stood and stared.

Oh my God! This is the worst thing in the world. Not only have I been really disrespectful, OUT LOUD, totally shaming, I've also shown myself to be just like my dad. It's exactly what he'd say. Hateful, horrid, despicable and total agony.

He wiped his nose on his sleeve.

Mole's grassed on my hidden need for a father figure, someone with authority, but I didn't want this one; a dad who behaves like this.

The whole room remained silent. Rows of faces fixed their eyes on Tony while Tony stared fixedly into space, as if all present were caught in a photograph. Then, through the silence, a scuttering in the eaves caused some silt from the river to fall through a crack in the ceiling. Like a shower of moon dust, each tiny particle glittered in the warm glow of candlelight, as it drifted through the rafters, delicately dusting the surfaces below.

Tony remained pale and motionless, like a ghost that had seen itself. During this moment, this beat in time, a grey bird with a cherry red tail, swooped down from the eaves in a swift and graceful arc. The silky brush of the parrot's wing gently skimmed the side of Tony's face. Without a sound, the bird rose, continuing its long and elegant arc, and before anyone had really noticed, the bird had ascended into the eaves and was gone.

Blinking, Tony touched his cheek and woke up.

'Doesn't anyone care about this boy?' he asked, in a low, clear voice. The silence in the room fizzed like static, whilst all faces at the elevated table stared ahead. One student began to sniff tearily into her handkerchief. Tony pointed to the rusty bolt, still sticking out of the table leg.

'Why hasn't anyone done anything about that bolt?' No one moved and no one made a murmur. 'This boy's face is gashed open and he's BLEEDING. Does anybody care?'

His voice rang out across the hall, quavering slightly as anxiety snatched his breath away. Touching his cheek again, he managed to get the fear under control.

Calm, calm.

Gripping the edge of the table for support, the wetness of his palms slid against the solidness of the wood. With a head about to burst, he screwed up his eyes to relieve the pressure; but not before catching sight of Mrs Sherbet popping something small into her mouth. Transfixed, he glimpsed pure terror on the face of the headmistress before she hid behind her water glass.

What was that? She just slipped something into her mouth and it definitely wasn't a pineapple chunk, she just took a pill or something…what else could it be?

Mrs Sherbet put down her glass and resumed a flat, blank expression. Tony felt himself shudder.

Focus, focus.

'Do you care about your students at all?' said Tony.

'Ouch,' said Nelson, as Bobbi dabbed his bleeding wound. Mrs Basher mumbled something about a plaster and a first aid box and ambled off.

All eyes remained on Mrs Sherbet, who now appeared remarkably poised, her gaze fixed on Tony. After a moment she leaned across and whispered something to Prospect, who gave a little nod. Mrs Sherbet stood up, patted her gull's egg and addressed the hall.

'Students and friends of Ellodian,' she said. 'We have heard what Mr Tony Plumb has got to say. Now, Mr Rownbout.'

Rownbout who was hovering behind the potted leylandii (destined for tinsel), stood up straight immediately, as if just whacked with a lithesome sapling.

'This is your fault entirely,' she said.

Everyone turned and Rownbout looked like he might collapse under the weight of the allegation. Mrs Sherbet continued.

'Now that lunch is over, I'm sure we're all eager to get back to our activities,' and with that she shot up from her seat and left the dining hall like a speedboat, Prospect bobbing in her wake.

Tony held his churning belly and tried to stop the tremor in his knees. He turned to Gaskin, who'd put his helmet back on and was halfway under the table.

Tony's shoulders drooped as he let out a heavy sigh.

You're not happy about Mrs Sherbet's response, grassed the excavator of the hidden mind.

'I'm not happy with your response,' shouted Tony after Mrs Sherbet's small entourage, but the shout was weak and they'd already gone.

The Christmas lunch broke up and he tried to share an exasperated look with Gaskin, but Gaskin scuttled off.

Christmas fun time over, it seems.

Tony made his way to the exit. Filing out slowly with all the rest, a couple of students patted him on the back.

'Look guys, I know I've not grasped the nettle properly. I let something slip through my fingers there. I should have said...'

'Sssh! – you shouldn't have said *anything*,' said someone.

'Rules, rules, rules,' said someone else.

Tony caught sight of Bobbi leaning against the wall; her face seemingly inhabited by newly arrived guests; the eye daggers of disdain, the lips of loathing and the complexion of colossal contempt.

She's deffo not going to smile back. Please say something nice to me. Hey, I'm coming over, maybe I'll say something nice to you?

But before he got the chance, she pushed off from the wall, flicked her hair and moved down the corridor with the others.

Guilt covered his entire being, like a big prickly cloak.

No wonder she doesn't like me now. Who would, if I'm so like my out of control dad?

Feeling queasy and burning hot, he started back along the shrubby corridor to his room. 'Flippin' heck,' he whispered, 'that was so not like me.'

...but it was you. So, are you in fact, just like your dad?

'No way!' he shouted and pulling a clod of earth out of the wall, threw it to the ground and stamped on it.

Fifteen

Nursing a gnawing headache, Tony wandered to the natural light that played on the walls of certain corridors and pushing open a creaky window, climbed through.

I reckon Ellodian's a massive maze and these little windows opening out directly onto the river, are probably the reason Ellodian floods from time to time. So how come these windows have never been blocked up? Hmm, maybe the natural light's precious, worth a flood or two and more important than being holed up and in the dark.

Standing on a particularly wonky little balcony, he gazed out over the river. The wintry landscape stood bleak and soggy; the nibbled ground drab and brown after the snow's retreat. A chilly breeze rustled through the grass and lifting his visor he took a deep breath of fresh air and his headache began to ebb away.

Just below him, where the water lapped against the side of the bank, the stubby vegetation of the previous summer lay in various stages of collapse, splashed with silt and stained streaky grey. He let his gaze travel down the river and saw a heron, completely still, but ready to strike. The force of the river had scooped out several water holes, small pools where the bank bulged, the water slowed and the brown fish gathered. In a pool close to Tony, the predator concentrated on catching a meal.

That heron's almost unreal, it's so poised, so completely quiet. Imagine being able to concentrate like that. The only sound's the river, popping and chuckling, and those chattering reeds, gossiping and whispering in the breeze. But they're not whispering anything bad about me or my parents; they're just rustling reeds. I know that. Coolio.

A flock of water birds suddenly batted the air with a ripple of soft applause and took flight. Black dots danced against the flat grey sky, their wobbly reflection mirrored in the colourless pools below.

The water's incredibly deep in parts, I bet there are beasts, like crocodiles, cutting through the weedy currents. I can almost see their backs and snouts, just breaking the surface, picked out by spots of light. Maybe these crocs hunt beneath the ripples? Maybe their tails cause those white foamy bubbles on the surface?

Suddenly a flowery scent crept around the edges of his helmet and he turned to see Bobbi Appledown smiling an apricot smile.

'Hello, Tony,' she said, and glancing around lifted her visor.

Calm, calm.

'Hi, Bobbi, how're you doin'?'

Her smile's so nice, I really like her but there's something about her that doesn't feel truly OK; like the way she spoke to Vicky when I first met her f'rinstance, that was completely uncool, and her rebuff after the Christmas lunch hurt a lot.

He glanced across at her brown eyes and smiled; she'd sought him out now though and that felt good.

She's forgiven.

'Did you get my Christmas card?' she asked, her cheeks pink.

'Umm, I did,' he said, 'thanks.' *That was another thing, there wasn't much encouragement in 'Merry Christmas' was there?*

'Did you look inside the card?'

'Er, yes, Merry Christmas, it said. I had to guess who it was from.' Tony kicked a stone from the balcony, into the river.

'Oh!' said Bobbi, 'yes, you must have been confused. Ha ha! I can see now what has happened Ha ha! – there's been a mistake. I have obviously, stupidly, sent you the wrong card. Yes – that's it.'

'Why are you laughing like that? You sound odd.'

Bobbi's face went red.

'Ha ha ha! I've probably sent your card to someone else, and you've got the card I should have sent to… er…my aunt.'

'Ah, I got you,' said Tony.

This story's deffo dodgy.

'So, there's someone out there who's got a magnificent and stunningly brilliant card. MY magnificent and stunningly brilliant card,' said Tony.

'Er…Yes, yes,' said Bobbi, flustered. '…But the chances are I didn't sign that either, so all will be OK…I think…I hope.' She smiled. 'So, if you want to give me that one back…I'll make it up to you with another card – at another time.'

Bobbi did something funny with her eyes that made them dance like feathery moths around a light bulb.

'Give it back?' he said, puzzled. 'Shouldn't I just throw it away?'

'Oh fine, absolutely fine…that's fine…' Bobbi's voice rose to a Gaskinesque squeak as she leant forward on the balcony, clutching a vine tightly as if she might fall over.

'Are you all right?'

'Ha ha ha…fine, absolutely fine…Ha ha…' Bobbi swayed about.

'Mrs Sherbet's asked me to tea. Has she asked you as well?' said Tony.

Bobbi stopped swaying and stared at him, as if she'd just taken a slap across the face. The moment hung in the air like the lingering smell from his bedroom sink. Tony shrugged, cheeks burning.

Tony you're feeling uneasy, ask yourself why this is. You know that she's going to flounce off now. Do you think you've said something that has upset her? Don't ignore this kind of behaviour Tony; ask her what's going on.

'What's the matter?' he said quietly.

'Nothing.'

'Will you still be here next year?'

'Er, not sure yet,' she said and with that she flicked down her visor and turned to leave the balcony, but Tony caught hold of her arm.

'What's going on Bobbi?' He spoke with a clear, deep tone. She pushed him away, her eyes wild and full of fear.

'While we're on the subject of what's going on, I have another question I've wanted to ask for ages. Prospect said there's room for thirty students here, but I've been counting, Bobbi, and excluding the friends who are older adults, I have never counted any more than twenty-nine students.'

'You must have made a mistake,' said Bobbi, her cheeks visibly wet and shiny, even through her visor.

'No, I haven't, I've been counting every morning at assembly for weeks and there are definitely twenty-nine. C'mon Bobbi, who and where is the thirtieth student?'

Sixteen

The winter sun danced and played with the early morning shadows, making circular patterns of light on his bedroom floor.

Pushing his long ginger fringe out of his eyes, he sat up in bed.

Yesterday's liaison with Bobbi troubled him, but he wasn't sure why. His mole was right, he did feel uneasy around Bobbi.

There definitely is something odd about her, despite her laughter and greetings card.

Pulling back the bedclothes he reached over to his desk and fished out her card from a pile of papers.

'Here it is, the card that's meant for someone else.'

Taking it from its envelope he fell back into bed and saw two pieces of coloured paper slip to the floor. Leaning over, he picked them up. One was a map of some description, the other a note, which said;

*Hello! I wonder if you would like to come out for lunch
with me? I know how to get a takeaway so that
Mrs Sherbet or anyone else doesn't know.
Here's a map that tells you how to get to The
Scrumptious Sausage.
Let me know if you would like to come.
Love Bobbi*

x

*LOVE BOBBI! Who was she writing to? Inviting that
person out to 'The Scrumptious Sausage' and sending love
and kisses? My aunt, huh!*

All the newfound confidence he'd experienced
when talking to Bobbi on the balcony, completely
evaporated.

'There am I, thinking this girl's really special,
finding out about her lip gloss, hoping to be her pal
even when she was rotten to Vicky, then discovering,
according to her, that she's sent me the wrong card, and
then I find this.'

He slapped the map down on the edge of his desk.

'So, who was this card meant to go to? "LOVE
Bobbi", it says.'

Tony curled his lip.

'It seems to me,' he snarled, 'that Bobbi Appledown
might have several boyfriends.'

*You don't know that she has several boyfriends and anyway
what if she has? You're angry that she said this card was not
for you.*

'Hmm. Well, she's deffo got her sights set on more than one boy and if that's the case, and I don't need help from you with this one, thank you Mole, I need to watch out or I'll seem a complete dingbat.'

No wonder she wanted the card back! The little fox just worked out she'd put this map and invitation in by mistake and wanted to hide her tracks. Is this the way girls work?

Tony whistled, shook his head and reached for his coat.

If you ask me, this is nothing short of a monstrous betrayal. I'm going to find her, right now, and confront her. I'll insist she tell me…What's that?

A muffled drumming fluttered up beneath the rug. Stopping at the door to listen, he stared as the rug twitched. Throwing it back he found the mole, visible from his tummy up and blinking in the skylight's wintry sunshine.

''Ello sir, 'ow 've you been? Now I've spoken to the missus about that there suggestion of yours, and she says to me to get myself right round 'ere and ask you to come for tea. Sorry it's taken so long, I've had problems with my top soil; storage, 'n' that.'

The mole reached in his pocket and pulled out a crumpled piece of paper. 'Now, let me see 'ere, what else 'ave I got to ask you. Ah yes, 'ere we go. She says the first thing to tell you is that you'll be welcome, that she'll be baking apple and blackberry crumble and is that all right, and what time would you like to come? Oh, and would the 18th at four o'clock be convenient?'

Tony glanced at his calendar and saw that he was due to have tea with Mrs Sherbet on the 19th.

'Fantastic! Thanks a lot, crumble's totally ace.'

'Aye well, I'll be getting off,' said the mole and began to descend.

'Wait!' said Tony, 'Where d'you live?'

'Oooh, now you're askin' me,' said the mole, lifting his little chequered cap and scratching his head. 'It i'n't that I don't know 'ow to get to me own 'ouse you understand, it's just workin' out the best way to tell you 'ow to get there, if you get me meaning. Now let me think.'

The mole rubbed his nose and a tiny pile of soil fell on the floor. Clearly in deep concentration he made some left and right movements with his paws in the air, as if waving down a plane. He then turned abruptly forty-five degrees.

'Aye,' he said to himself, 'that's right.' He turned to Tony. 'Now do you know where the "Bull and Bush" is?'

'Er – no.'

'Right,' said the mole 'that in't a problem, let me think.' He stroked his chin. 'Do you know Chip Parker's betting office?'

'Sorry.'

'Do you know anywhere 'ere abouts then?'

'…Well, I know where "The Scrumptious Sausage" is, at least I've got a map.'

'That's it then,' said the mole, 'you've cracked it. We live 'round the corner and two doors down.'

Tony offered the mole the map, and drawing a pencil out from beneath his cap, the mole put a wobbly cross about an inch away from 'The Scrumptious Sausage'.

'There you go sir, Ivy Grove, number five,' said the small furry mammal, pushing the pencil back into his cap. 'You can't go wrong. Just stay this side of the river and go down the steps. At the large stone, follow this map and you'll be with us in no time. I'll tell the missus to expect you.' The mole prepared to go.

'What's your name, please?'

The mole gave a little laugh and climbed back out of the hole, pattered up toward Tony and offered out his paw.

'Frank Cubbage,' said the mole. 'Pleased to meet you.'

Tony fell back on his pillows and smiled. *A betting mole that goes to the 'Bull and Bush'. He might have got on with my dad.*

Seventeen

At four o'clock Tony rapped on the door of number five Ivy Grove.

'I'll get it,' came a voice from inside. The door sprang open and Tony peered into an empty hallway.

A small brown and pink face slowly emerged from behind the door.

'Are you Mr Tony Plumb?'

'Yes, I am.'

'Please will you come in, I'm Jasper Cubbage aged seven.'

Tony grinned at Jasper and entered the house.

'This is our sitting room; that's the kitchen – Mum's in there – that's where we eat.'

'Fab,' said Tony, swooning in the delicious aroma.

'Well hello,' said a friendly voice. A plump mole with a ribbon around her polished head, came bustling into the room. 'Tony Plumb,' she said, 'welcome to our home,' and wiping her hands on her apron she shook

Tony's hand. 'I'm Mrs Cubbage, but please call me Ethel, this is Jasper.'

Jasper rushed to sit on the flowery sofa and appeared to be engrossed in a magazine, as if the event of having a stranger to tea happened all the time. From the welcoming atmosphere, Tony believed it probably did. Jasper flicked the magazine with benign indifference, disguising an eagerness revealed only by the fact that he peeped out from behind the pages every other second, watching Tony's every move.

'Hello,' said Tony. 'I met Jasper at the door, he let me in.'

From the edge of his eye Tony could see Jasper's grin.

'Good. Frank's just nipped out with Emily, our daughter, she's thirteen.'

'I'm not sure if I've done the right thing,' Tony hesitated, 'I've brought you a gift.'

'I didn't expect that!' she said accepting the package, 'thank you.'

The delighted mole peered into the bag. 'HAND CREAM,' she squealed, 'and nail revitaliser! Wait 'til I show Frank. It's perfect. You're so thoughtful.'

Mrs Cubbage planted a kiss on Tony's cheek. He was surprised but quite flattered. Her little mouth felt as soft as velvet.

Frank and Emily came back with a bottle of wine and two large bags of salt and vinegar crisps. Mrs Cubbage put the crisps into bowls and Tony and Jasper ate them all in the space of two minutes.

'Typical,' said Emily, 'good job I've hidden the other bag. Mum, Dad, you'd better have some crisps and quick! We're in the presence of gannets.'

'Are there shops near Ellodian?' said Tony, eyeing the crisps.

Emily nodded, mid-nibble.

''Ello, sir,' said a smiling Frank Cubbage, taking off his jacket, 'welcome to our home. I could show you my garden later if you like, or now, if you prefer.'

Picking up on the cue, Tony followed Frank out through the back door to a plot of land about thirty feet square, which like the front garden, was simply soil.

'Very er…good…er, I mean nice,' said Tony, glad at least that there were no complicated plants requiring identification.

'Top soil,' said Frank scratching his head and replacing his cap. 'The works department, minor buildin' works, repairs, that sorta thing is my other job 'ere at Ellodian' (he pronounced it "Hello Diane"). 'But this 'ere's my natural gift.'

Tony nodded.

'The truck comes in 'ere,' said Frank, putting out both paws, 'and reverses into that spot there.' The mole set off along a path, at speed. ''Ere,' he said, 'is where we load up. Takes five-ton o' top soil at a time and we can prepare about ooooh, let me see, about ten ton a day with me, Ethel and Jasper. Me brother Ernie gives us an 'and. Now Emily, she does a bit but it's 'er age the

114

missus says and that she'll be better after adolescence. 'Ave you 'eard of adolescence?' Frank pronounced it 'add 'n' lessen'.

'Adolescence? Well, yes,' said Tony. 'It's quite normal y' know for a young person to go through adolescence.'

Frank stopped abruptly. 'Is it?' he said, facing his new friend.

'Oh yes, it's usual for young people in their teenage years or adolescence to go through phases. Sometimes they, I mean we, go through stages of discontent.'

A loud and energetic conversation with a social worker three years ago, drifted back into mind: 'Tony, I must warn you, discontent is the devil's friend.' He hadn't forgotten about discontent.

I wonder if I still harbour discontent?

'I'm probably still an adolescent myself,' he said, looking at the soil.

'You? Oh no,' said Frank Cubbage. 'I've got you down as a young man, a chap y'know, like meself… grateful, like me, for the life you've got and hopeful for what's to come.'

As Frank's words sank in, Tony blinked and studied the progress of an ant as it lugged a particle of soil, four times bigger than itself, to some important destination.

'Tea's ready,' shouted Mrs Cubbage.

'There we go,' said Frank, 'we've been looking forward to this y'know.'

Tony smiled. Returning to the kitchen, he luxuriated in the warm scents of home; wood smoke, polish and hyacinths in a pretty bowl, wafting alongside the delicious smells of good home cooking. Everyone gathered and sat down.

'Why is the dictionary to be relied upon?' said Emily tucking a napkin under her chin.

'Because you can squash a vole with it,' said Jasper.

'No, because moles come first, before stoats, voles and weasels.'

Mrs Cubbage tutted. 'You'll think us terrible Tony,' she said. 'We're not very politically correct. That'll do now, our Emily.'

'Ah stuff and nonsense,' said Frank pouring out wine for everyone, including a small glass for Jasper, to which Mrs Cubbage added a drop of water.

'Could I have a bit more wine please?' asked Emily.

'It's a drop more, Emily not a bit. You can't have a bit of liquid. I don't know Dad; can our Emily have a bit more wine?' Mrs Cubbage bustled back into the kitchen.

'Well I suppose just a little tot then. No more mind. We don't want you getting tiddly.'

Emily's nose turned crimson.

'Pass yer glass,' said Frank.

'No thank you,' she said in a high-pitched voice. 'I've changed my mind. I don't want any more wine.'

'Why's that then?' said Jasper.

'Bee-cause,' hissed his sister, 'it isn't very ladylike.' Emily sat up very straight in her chair.

'But you're not a lady,' hissed Jasper, 'you're a mole.'

'I know I'm a mole silly, but I'm a lady mole.'

A heavy numbness rapidly settled around Tony as he eyed the wine bottle, but the sheer pleasure on the faces of the Cubbage family, their warm and generous smiles and all the giggling soon chased the numbness away. He took a sip of the wine, it tasted light and bouncy on his tongue.

Frank chortled at Emily's comment as Mrs Cubbage placed a bowl of steaming stew in the centre of the table.

Tony inhaled.

I'm in heaven.

'A toast to good manners,' said Frank, beaming. Tony chuckled and raised his glass. The stew smelled totally yummy and after the boring soup at Ellodian his mouth began to water. Heaping crispy golden potatoes onto his plate he sighed and reckoned that the Cubbages were a family who truly enjoyed their food. Emily waved a carrot at Tony.

'Home grown,' she said.

Empty plates began to gather.

Tony leaned back from the table. 'I didn't realise how hungry I was, that was by miles the best meal I've had in years, maybe ever.'

'I hope you've left room,' said Mrs Cubbage gathering herself and heading to the oven, returning with a blackberry-and-apple crumble and a large jug of custard.

After dinner Frank and Tony washed up, Jasper put the crockery in the cupboard and Emily put the kettle on. Mrs Cubbage sat down on the flowery sofa. One by one the family joined her in the sitting room.

Frank put on his spectacles and taking Tony's gift from the sideboard, began to study the label, interrupting the conversation to say things like; 'This 'as got Benzyl Salicylate in it.'

Jasper giggled and read his magazine.

Tony felt good, calm and in the best mood for ages.

So, this is what being in a family is really like.

———✦✦✦———

Waving goodbye to the Cubbages, he heard the door of number five click shut, and as he turned, the first thing he noticed was a carpet and the second thing was a sign hanging from the ceiling that said: 'Evensham Social Services Children's Department'.

'Aaooww!' He felt a sharp pain. It was too dark to see anything properly, but his hand felt sticky and wet. Moving to a window, light shone in from the street.

Blood.

Looking down, there was glass on the lino floor. The clock above the reception desk said two-thirty.

I think I can safely say that's two-thirty am. What's that?

A light was flicking on and off in the corner of the foyer. Moving towards it, he yanked on some wires: the pip, pip, pip sound stopped, and the burglar alarm box almost fell off the wall.

Ah, dear social services, once in a while you should treat your antiques to an overhaul.

Rubbing his hand on his tee shirt, he looked about. Aided by shafts of light from outside, he picked out a whiteboard on the opposite wall. Names, room numbers and a column that said IN/OUT were handwritten, almost illegibly, in marker pen. Tony ran his eye down the smudgy squiggles.

Bendy, Bendy, Bendy. There she is. Room 10a. Good job I've been here before.

Up the stairs, two at a time, Tony turned left into an open space with doors along one side.

10a where are you? Gotcha!

Tony squeezed the door handle.

Locked.

Turning around he eyed the desks, silent in the semi-dark, like sprawling off-duty soldiers, sleeping in barracks. Suddenly he felt his breath halt in his throat. A cone of bright light partially illuminated one of the desks at the back of the room. Was someone there? Someone sitting quietly at a desk in the middle of the night?

I can't see you, but can you see me?

A car horn hooted from the street below and he almost fell over. In a section of his mind, the distant rumble of thought chariots began, but Tony found their brakes when he realised someone had forgotten to switch off their desk lamp.

His breath slowly left his chest.

Keep calm, Plumb, there is no one here, you're OK. Go to the desk. The desk. Calm, calm.

A bright yellow scarf hung over the back of the chair. In the centre of the desk, amid papers, a mug of milk-less tea and an A-Z of Evensham, was a note.

```
Hi Bendy,
   Your referral letter for TP
is done and just needs you to
sign. I've clipped it to the
original report, which I pulled
out of the file for reference.
They can both go back into
his file on Monday when you've
signed. The letter and report
are in my drawer.
   Sorry it's taken so long.
   See you Monday,
   Ellie
```

'Ellie, Ellie, flowery Ellie, sweet and oh so smelly – I know exactly where your desk is and if you've not changed your routine, I also know where you keep the key to your drawer.'

Tony leapt down the stairs to the foyer thinking for the first time that all the waiting around in reception with nothing to do but watch the admin staff, was about to pay off big time. Checking a small room to his left, he grinned broadly at the glowing red lights of the office photocopier.

Eighteen

What? morning already?

Kicking off his bed covers, Tony dressed, ran to grab some bread from the dining hall and breathlessly wiping the crumbs from his mouth, banged on Mrs Heapey's door.

She won't mind that it's not my proper appointment time.

He thumped the door again.

Where is she?

Several young saplings, their roots springing from beneath a rock, grew horizontally before their boughs twisted upwards to reach a crevice of light. This survival tactic on the part of the young trees had formed a sort of seat, and although tipped at an angle, it was good enough. Tony sat down on a bough to wait.

Maybe Mrs Heapey had gone away on holiday or was ill and wasn't coming back for ages?

She can't be available all the time Tony, she's got her own life to lead y'know.

The prospect of not seeing her for weeks descended like a damp winter fog. He sighed and slid off the tree.

'Tony!' Mrs Heapey appeared around a curve in the corridor, bags and files in hand. His heart calmed.

As she got closer, he sensed she might hug him. When it didn't happen he steadied himself, his skin prickling with coolness. *She wants to hug me, of course she does, but she can't because she's carrying files and stuff.*

Mrs Heapey opened the door to her room.

'Don't you live here then?' he asked. Mrs Heapey didn't answer.

Putting her bags down on her desk, she led Tony through to the room with the comfy chairs where they usually sat.

'I have to admit,' she said settling into her chair, 'I was concerned about you when you didn't turn up for your last appointment.'

'I can't believe it myself really, but I forgot.' Mrs Heapey looked at him.

I'm blushing, she can see I am.

Mrs Heapey maintained her thoughtful gaze.

Say it.

'Well the truth is, seeing that brandy bottle on your fireplace made me think you drank a lot. It reminded me of…and er, well…'

You were angry and worried that brandy bottle meant Mrs Heapey wasn't going to be a reliable adult.

'You might be a drinker…'

'Like your mother?'

'Mmm, I worried that I probably couldn't rely on you either.' Tony sniffed and scanned the room. 'Also, it smelled a bit funny in here last time, but that seems to have gone now.' Tony hoped Mrs Heapey might offer an explanation.

The turquoise orbs were steady.

Tony blinked. '...But, I got you a Christmas card. Um, it's all bent and battered and a bit late. Sorry.'

Smiling, she thanked him and put it on the mantelpiece. The brandy bottle had vanished. A small darkening cloud hovered in the atmosphere, just above Tony's head.

Hang on, that smile she's giving me doesn't look real. Is it painted on? She looks like she's made of plastic.

The outline of Mrs Heapey's face developed small multiple edges, like separate static images from a continuous film and when she moved, the frozen outlines followed her as if trying to reunite with her body.

A shiver wriggled down his back.

Calm, calm.

An unwanted vision of Mrs Heapey stepping out from a chariot sprang up before him. Wrapped in a black fur cloak, her face was as white as the moon. Her mouth, a gash of red remained fixed, while her laser-like eyes swept over him, intent on finding some choice morsel of the Tony Plumb kind; something to satisfy an appetite too gruesome to imagine. Tony blinked and shook the image off.

Get a grip, she's my friend. He steadied himself.

'You're going to tea with Mrs Sherbet, this afternoon I think you said?' Her solid outline was reinstated and her voice gentle, but a steely chip, a fragment of something hard and clear, glinted in the corner of her eye.

'That's tonight. I don't really know what to expect.' Tony snatched a peek at her from under his fringe. Her face now held a healthy glow and she seemed more like her old self; warm and kind and interested, not plastic, not multiple and her mouth wasn't red anymore.

The turquoise eyes twinkled.

She's fine, I trust her and...

You're going to say this anyway...here it comes...

'Erm, there's something I need to tell you. I'm not sure what's happening but I've been out. Twice,' said Tony.

'Out?'

'Yes. Outside, and sometimes, I feel a bit, well, I'm not sure how to describe it really. Things seem to change and change quick, and my mind's a bit like spaghetti. Then there's the thought chariots.'

'Thought chariots?' Mrs Heapey leaned in.

'Don't worry, it doesn't matter. At first, I thought it was wacky here but safe, now I'm not so sure. There's a lot of time wasted and sometimes it feels like things don't get tackled. Like life's a melting candle, and I don't know if there're any more candles in the box. I know I'm here to do something, something important. It's deffo about those three questions I told you about, and my past.'

'Yes.'

'But it's also about being here, there's something

going on here at Ellodian, something really weird, and I need to sort that out too.'

'Tony,' said Mrs Heapey, 'sometimes we keep things separate from other things in our mind, to help us to cope, even when really they're all connected.'

'Hmm. But what happened in my past is deffo separate from what's happening here, at Ellodian. I mean, c'mon, Mrs Sherbet isn't my mum, now is she? Take a break on that one Mrs Heapey, will you?'

'Maybe not Mrs Sherbet, but a moment ago you thought I drank like your mum and might be unreliable too.'

'Hmm,' said Tony. His eyes flicked sideways.

'But you're saying, Tony, that you think there is something weird here, something you can't fathom?'

He caught her sharp look.

It's OK, she's still normal. She's here to help and I trust her.

Great idea.

'Sometimes I'm scared, really scared,' said Tony.

Eventually Mrs Heapey spoke.

'I guess sometimes we don't know what to do with our fear.'

'You know when I spoke about my mum?'

Moving back to talk about your mum and dad is a relief, an escape from this stealing evil presence that's choking the air in the room, share your worries; is Mrs Heapey really on your side, do you really trust her?

OK Mole, not now and yes, I do!

125

Just saying.

Mrs Heapey nodded. 'Yes, you spoke about your mum.'

'Well,' his voice wavered slightly 'I do accept she was a drug addict. Once she nearly fell out of the bedroom window after smoking something, and too much beer.'

'So, you're ready to give up on the idea that your mother was perfect?'

'Yes,' said Tony, letting out a harboured breath.

'My parents,' he said slowly, 'were unstable and in a mad – crazy – moment, they convinced each other that the best thing to do was to jump off a waterfall and leave me on my own. They were j-junkies.'

Tears welled in his eyes, but taking a tissue and blowing his nose, he carried on.

'They didn't deserve to be my parents.' A hard lump began to expand in his throat. 'I still love my mum, but now I've got you, I think it might be easier to let her go, if you know what I mean.' Tony raised his eyes to meet hers.

Mrs Heapey looked directly back. 'Separating from your mum has been difficult because the relationship must have been fraught with anxiety, and because you haven't had a dad you could go to and look up to.'

'He should look up to me,' said Tony, his eyes fierce as he pointed at his chest. 'I am better than him.'

Fixing him with her turquoise gaze, she moved slightly forward. 'It sounds like you think your dad was completely useless and yet he took you to the cinema, he took you to the zoo, and he introduced you to moles.

From what I can see, your understanding of the internal mole, the one you told me about that grasses on the bits of your mind that you have been keeping secret from yourself, is a wonderful idea. This is a gift that perhaps you wouldn't have discovered, if it wasn't for your dad. He was human you know, as human as your mum was. They were together in what they decided to do.'

Wow, that's the longest speech she's ever made.

His eyes shot to the little chink of daylight knifing through the curtains and his heart began to hammer.

No! Don't push this away – she says your dad was human; he was human so, despite your upset with him and your hatred of the things he did, he was capable of relationships. He had a relationship with your mum. Yes! They were lovers, husband and wife. Partners in crime but partners none-the-less. You're seeing now that you weren't a part of what they had, their sharing, their togetherness and...aaaarghh!

Does she actually know how miserable it is to be an outsider and feel unwanted and unimportant? Has she ever been left alone, locked in a shower room for three whole hours, shoved in a cupboard or just ignored for weeks on end? I don't think she's a monster spook, I think she really does want to help, but she's digging a bit too deep here.

Hey, don't knock digging. You're right Tony, she isn't a monster or a spook, but she's definitely challenging your ideas about Mum and Dad...

'I guess you're wondering if I can understand how it feels to be pushed out or excluded? If I can understand what it's like to feel at the mercy of those in authority? I guess Daisy Bank didn't help.'

'Get lost,' said Tony quietly.

Mrs Heapey went on.

'Maybe even worse than realising your parents were a couple and loved each other, is the prospect that they didn't really want you.'

Mrs Heapey's voice was slow and steady. Her turquoise eyes held him in her gentle gaze. Tony gave her a look that would drill through brick, stood up and without speaking, walked to the door.

Mrs Heapey caught up with him.

'Oh, and Tony if you want to come back, please make an appointment first.' Her voice was kindly but firm.

'What happened to "I'll be here if you need me"?' he snarled, remembering the hundreds of times carers had uttered these words, before deserting him. 'I see that you don't want me either. Well, listen to me, I know what happened with my parents, I know all about it, so you can just go and boil your psychotherapy.'

Tony you've morphed into a white-faced plastic monster with blood on your mouth...

Walking straight back to his room he rammed home the wooden bolt, flung himself on his bed and cried and cried and cried.

Nineteen

C'mon now Tony, that bit about knowing what happened with your parents wasn't strictly true was it?

Do you have to know everything, Mole?

Reaching under his bed for his rucksack, he pulled out the photocopies he'd taken from Bendy's office. Holding the paper still was impossible; the thought chariots broke free and smashed by, brandishing old threats and carrying ancient demons. Worms escaped from cans, cats jumped out of bags, spilled beans bounced everywhere, and the mole hobnobbed on and on, until Tony's head threatened to explode.

Please let me read this, let me read this and know. I NEED TO KNOW.

The words on the page were mobile and seemed to dance about. Letters jumped off the page, jumping back somewhere else, making new words that didn't make sense.

Shoving the papers back into his rucksack Tony sensed that now was not the time.

Twenty

So, tea at the Sherbet's. Can't believe how nervous I am.
I've got butterflies about going there, and worse, that
sweaty finger of fear, the one that started prodding me
the moment I got here, still jabs me in the chest. There's
deffo something about Ellodian I can't fathom. What did
McGurney say? Question Ellodian? Hello Ellodian, how
come you're such a weird and kooky place?

What if Mrs Sherbet's another so-called adult who doesn't
want me either? Or maybe this invitation's just a trap? I
could be captured and held prisoner at Ellodian forever.

Maybe Mrs Heapey and Mrs Sherbet are colluding?
Scheming together, two evil witches cooking up a plan —
something monstrous, diabolical, a sinister plot to get rid
of me. That cold, steely glint in Mrs Heapey's eye when I
mentioned going to Sherbet's for tea. Double bubble, toilet
trouble. That's what the witches at Daisy Bank used to say.
I don't want to get plonked in double doo doo; a Heapey-
Sherbet collaboration for hellish tricks and torture.

Standing up straight, he shifted his thoughts to something good.

The Cubbages wanted me. Maybe this tea party's a chance for Mrs Sherbet to show she approves of me too? As for Mrs Heapey, she wouldn't relish evil doing.

'No,' he muttered 'not Mrs Heapey, definitely not Mrs Heapey.'

Striding through the corridors, a large weeping willow forced him to turn left. Alongside the path ahead, the stooping teacher with leaves still in his hair let himself into a large, grand residence with a bright yellow door.

This must be the posh bit of Ellodian.

Picking his way over some damp ground, he came to a grove where silver birch saplings grew close together, their intertwining trunks skimming the face of a rocky escarpment. Wooden planks formed a raised walkway above the grove's soggy earth and led Tony to Mrs Sherbet's door.

Breathe, breathe, breathe. What time is it? One-minute past four. This crash helmet's really tight. I hope I can take it off, once I'm inside.

The house had a stone front and was built back into the rock. It had a proper panelled front door, painted gloss black, with a large brass knocker in the centre. Raising the knocker, he let it fall and a low dull noise bounced off the escarpment and echoed around the copse.

Who else is going to be here? Surely not just me and Sherbet – perish that thought for starters.

He took another deep breath. The drifting sourness of the muddy grove made the hair in his nostrils tingle.

OK, someone's coming.

The door creaked slowly open and there was Prospect, minus his gown and dressed in a roomy grey jumper, a sandy coloured shirt and a pair of dark grey trousers.

'Come in dabster,' said Prospect offering Tony a baggy smile, which soon collapsed into the sallow folds of his skin.

Tony stepped over the threshold. He smiled back at Prospect. 'Hello.'

Prospect turned and set off down a long stony corridor, before turning left to open a door.

Holey Emmental – this is bright!

Captured in a permanent flash of sheet lightning, the sitting room burned beneath a low ceiling crammed with fluorescent tubes. He blinked. Quite large and sparsely furnished, it had an enormous television and a sofa pushed up against the wall. All seating faced the electric fire and the TV.

A pop of orange colour caught his eye.

S'ppose that orange rug's quite cheery, but if it weren't for this damp musky smell, I'd think I was about to be fried in a fire pit. There's even growths, like mushrooms or cauliflowers coming out of the walls. Hmm. Those slimy growths could be quite cool and arty, like sculptures, except they stink of rotting cheese. The heat from these lights should be drying the place out, instead it's just cooking the toadstools.

A noisy clump, clumping announced the arrival of

Mrs Sherbet, who appeared with a large drink in hand. Tony caught a whiff.

Ugh! That drink's like lighter fuel. Funny, it's so different to the wine I tasted at the Cubbages.

Prospect circled on the spot, making little movements with his hands, as if to usher him further into the room.

'Hello Tony and welcome,' said Mrs Sherbet, in a voice that sounded like she was reading the football results. Her plump hand patted a cushion on the leathery sofa. Tony moved towards her to sit down, but immediately stepped back as the headmistress swung her bulk into the space, letting herself fall back onto the cushion with a resounding slap. 'Sit down,' she said. Her lips flew back to her glass. Tony glanced around.

'Anywhere,' she said waving her free arm randomly across the room

Prospect was still circling, trying to smile and mumbling a bit.

'Dabster, oh dabster, yes…er dabster.'

'Sorry, what?' said Tony, 'what does that word actually mean? Prospect gazed into the distance and smiled.

'It means dabster, that you are the expert, you are the dab hand, the resourceful one, and I, well I am, well, nothing of the sort…' Prospect turned away, any further insights lost in a mumble.

It's such a shame. I bet he's OK really, but he just seems so, reduced.

Tony's thought was cut short by Mrs Sherbet's announcement.

'Bobbi's already here,' said Mrs Sherbet. 'Oh, and I think you know Vicky.'

Tony spun around.

'Vicky?' He stared at the little figure entering the room. Everything went white for a second. Fighting an urge to go over and hug her, Tony said, 'I…I…er. I haven't seen you for a while.'

'Hello Tony, you're right, I've not been around much.'

Her nose quivered as she sat down on a dining chair and placed her small pink hands across her lap.

What on earth was she wearing? It resembled some sort of climbing frame, covered in frilly pink stuff.

'Your dress…?'

'A present. It's a crinoline.'

'Oh right.'

'I've been away on a course, courtesy of Sylvia.'

'Syl…?' he looked quickly at Mrs Sherbet and back at Vicky. Prospect continued to hover but made slow progress toward a chair.

'I'm going to be married.' Vicky smiled a tiny smile into the back of her hand and turned her head away daintily.

Prospect had positioned himself, feet slightly apart, and was about to fall back into the chair when Mrs Sherbet spoke sharply.

'Drinks, Prospect.' The thin grey man righted himself and set off, shuffling towards a wooden cabinet in the corner of the room. 'Prospect,' said Mrs Sherbet, 'is my husband.'

Tony reeled. He'd hoped Bobbi would be here, but Vicky? Not only here, but happy? And Prospect and Sherbet married? His knees buckled and he fell backwards, fortunately into a chair.

Mrs Sherbet rattled off some drinks.

'We have whisky and soda, brandy and babybubble, port and lemon, gin and tonic, cider and pineapple, rum and cherry cola, red wine and lemonade, beer with honey, white wine and vinegar and I think we have some vodka with garlic cream in there somewhere, is that right, Prospect?'

Tony felt his stomach roll.

'What do you want?' she asked.

The words 'To leave', headlined before his eyes.

'Erm, a lemonade would be good. Er…thanks.'

'What, just a lemonade?' Her eyes darted at him. 'Why not have a drink? Now is the cocktail hour and you aren't a baby.'

'Er…no thanks,' he said, not wanting to engage Mrs Sherbet in a conversation about thirteen being a bit young to glug whisky, 'I'll stick with the lemonade.' Her face darkened. Mrs Sherbet muttered something to Prospect.

The lights continued to broil the room. Tony removed his coat, putting it on the floor by his chair.

'Do you like poetry?' asked Vicky politely. Transferring his gaze to the tiny being, he could just about make out what she was saying through double visor vision. The foamy pinkness of her dress billowed out between them; a ridiculous giant cloud in comparison to her tiny feet, wrapped in silk slippers with ribboned bows bigger than her bones. Around her miniscule waist, a red sash terminated in another gargantuan bow.

'Umm…I'm not sure…I don't really know much poetry…' He remembered Miss Woosey's poem, 'When Pansies Burst…' or something like that but didn't think that's what Vicky meant.

'I can cook and sew and read poetry,' said Vicky. Tony got the distinct impression that her statement had been pre-prepared, but not by her.

'Your crash helmet…' Tony gestured to her head gear. 'Are you a student here?' Vicky turned her face to him. 'It's just that the day I saw you, in the dining hall, you wore Ellodian's uniform.'

…and you weren't acting dumb and affected like this.

'Best not to draw attention – don't you think?' was all she said.

'Aaah Vicky,' said Mrs Sherbet, 'so delicious in pink and such a little princess. Soon your suitor will come.'

This is completely creepy, she's not a helpless child.

Vicky played up to it, dipping her head prettily and emitting something between a cry of delight and a giggle.

This play-acting's totally weird. Is she unstable or

drugged or something? It's as if she's in the room, and yet at the same time, she's not really here at all.

'Who are you marrying, um, anyone I know…?'

'A perfect boy,' said Mrs Sherbet breezily, thrusting her fist into a bowl of prawn crackers.

Prospect handed him a glass full of fizzy brown liquid, which Tony took and put down on the floor by his coat.

'Fffzzz, fffzzz,' said Prospect and turned full circle.

A small noise behind him preceded Bobbi's entrance; who, even in her helmet, appeared queasy, uncomfortable and full of trepidation.

'Ah Bobbi,' said Mrs Sherbet, without even a glance, concentrating instead on pouring herself another drink. Bobbi seemed tense, as if she might cry.

Right this is coming off.

The yellow crash helmet bumped down on the floor. After a short silence, Bobbi removed hers and then Vicky, crying in delight, followed suit.

That's better, at least now I can breathe in this grilling heat. Hang on what's that funny noise?

Thump, thump, thump.

What's Mrs Sherbet doing with her eyes? They're rolling around like marbles on a dinner plate and how come she's started talking so loudly?

'Well,' hollered Mrs Sherbet, 'I guess as we're being friendly and sociable, we might as well relax.'

'Berser…err…er ser…' said Prospect and hiccupped.

A trail of heavy thumping punched its way across the ceiling.

Someone's upstairs. How come no one's saying anything? Can they hear it too?

And again; a loud thump and the sound of something breaking. Tony stiffened and looked at the others. Wasn't anyone going to notice and tell him what it was? It sounded like a trapped animal trying to get out.

'Aren't you going to drink your lemonade?' bellowed Mrs Sherbet. Tony stared at her, not knowing what to say.

'Erm…'

'Let's eat,' said Mrs Sherbet, heaving herself to a standing position. Waddling over to the table she began to fiddle with plates, keeping up a loud stream of chatter. Tony caught Bobbi's eye and she managed a watery smile.

This food's all a bit off colour. I mean, green custard tarts? Grey éclairs with maroon chocolate? Yellow bread and blue boiled ham? Ah, apples they're reddishly, greenishly normal.

Tony took one.

As people moved around the table he managed to sidle up to Vicky.

'How come you're here?'

'It's curious, don't you think, how there are always at least two sides to everyone and two sides, at least, to everything?'

'I don't know what you mean, but listen I'm trying to find a Mr Burrow, is he someone you know?'

'Why yes, of course Tony, don't you realise? He's the...'

Tony bit into a chocolate éclair. He didn't remember putting it on his plate. The pastry, a bite, the ceiling, those fluorescents. Spinning, spinning. Then black.

Twenty-One

Tony kept on spinning down a long dark tunnel. Images of Vicky, Bobbi, Mrs Sherbet, Prospect and Mr Burrow on the bank, floated up and then, like wisps of cold breath, just slipped away.

Bump! Oooof! What the...? I'm on a bobsleigh, wow, that's fast. The corridors of Ellodian; ooops, never been down this one before. Aaargh! My ears! What's that? Just sh-shapes and co-colours shooting past. I c-can't cling on much tighter, totally freaky; any second, I'll tip up and be mushed against the wall. Sweesh! Uh! Now what? What's happened? Everything's stopped and gone quiet.

That's Mrs Heapey's door. Where's the bobsleigh gone?

Tony pressed himself into a curtain of ivy as Mrs Heapey came along the corridor, heading for her room. Surprised at his agility Tony slid in after her but braked when he saw a pile of lumpy vomit on the floor. Side-stepping the smelly pile, he wriggled behind an armchair and hid.

'I'm here, you old Heap.'

The whiney voice was coming from the very chair he was hiding behind.

Crouching, he peeped out. The scene was edged in fuzziness, but he could make out Mrs Heapey sitting down in the opposite chair. Behind Mrs Heapey was a big blurry mirror.

Tony frowned.

That's new, how come I've not seen that before?

Peering into the mirror he recoiled. There in full vision, sat the occupant of the chair that hid him.

It's that boy, the greeny-grey boy who stinks like a drain.

Tony peeked again. The stench was horrible.

He doesn't seem to be wearing much and why doesn't he just have a wash? What's so scary about that?

Tony shuddered, remembering the white tiled showers at Daisy Bank. The faint image of a shower cubicle left Tony's mind strapped to the back of a speeding thought chariot.

Mrs Heapey was speaking. It sounded like she called the boy Perfect. From the cloudy image in the mirror it appeared he was eating something with legs, and now Mrs Heapey's breathing had changed, was she crying? Tony desperately wanted to comfort her but daren't move. Inching his knees sideways, he managed to get into a better position.

The boy belched loudly. 'Oh! Scouzie me.'

Mrs Heapey said something and, detecting the underlying chill of terror in her voice, he remembered where he'd seen the boy before. It was a time before Christmas. This was the boy who'd entered Mrs Heapey's rooms, just as he was leaving. *Rotting fish and bad eggs. Phworrr!* This wasn't Perfect at all, this boy was Perfax.

'He's drugged,' said Perfax, finishing the snack. 'Mummiedear has it all under control. She's got him, and she'll keep him until I say he can go.'

Mummiedear? – this horror is Mrs Sherbet's son?

'What do you want him for?' said Mrs Heapey.

Tony tried to focus.

The boy picked up a small trinket from the table and snapped it in two.

'Tony will be my friend. He'll teach me how to be… erm…plezzzant, y'know, cute. An irresistible hunny bunny, an adorable boy.'

Tony gasped.

Perfax threw the trinket over his shoulder. 'We all need good friends to help us, even me.' He let out a laugh that sounded like a dentist's drill.

'In fact, particularly me. He'll be the one to show me how to do things nicey-nicey, how to get people to do what I want. I will become royalty, a princey kingy thingy and the world will be mine to do with as I want. A husband to Her Royal Highness, the Princess Vicky, I will be King Perfax, ruler of Ellodian. Well that'll do me for now, but tomorrow it's King Perfax ruler of the world.'

The boy's cold dead eyes stared flatly ahead, suppressing any impulse Tony had to laugh out loud.

'But why drug him?' whispered the therapist.

Perfax rolled his tiny eyes 'Beeecause, beeecause, beeecause he mightn't do it, he mightn't be my special friend.'

'So, you need Tony to realise your dream?'

'I'm not stupid, Dung Heap, Tony Plumb has got something, a little spark of...' Perfax passed the fat, grey, toad of a tongue around his lipless mouth... 'that thing, what is it now? That thing he's got. He's got a little spark of goodness and that's what I'm after. I'll gouge it out of him and have it for myself.'

'Gouge? I mean, how do you imagine you'll get that from him?'

'Lordy me! You really are a bore sometimes Creepy Heapey. He'll hand it over, stupid, he'll coach me on what to say and do to make me a sweetie pie, a lovely young man with charm and POWER. He'll do this for me you see, because he believes it's good to be grateful for things and to help others. Though heaven only knows what he's got to be grateful for. Beats me.'

Perfax growled the last bit and made a fist with his hand. Thump! The chair wobbled.

'Yes, I think it does beat you, and tell me Perfax, what's so wrong with being grateful for things and wanting to help others?'

A silence descended. Managing to sneak just one eyeball around the edge of Perfax's chair, Tony glanced into the mirror and saw that Perfax had turned almost completely green.

'HE'S JUST SO NICE AND I CAN'T STAND IT. I've stood back and spied on him – he has friends and gets things. I don't know how he gets to be good, but I want to be good like that, I want it now, and you Poo Heap, will not interfere.'

'Or else?'

'Or else I will kill you.'

Mrs Heapey leaned forward. 'I think you've bullied me for too long, and now I'm going to act. You're a spoilt boy and you need lots of help, perhaps more than I have it in me to give, but I'm going to keep trying. The thing is Perfax you can't threaten to kill people or manipulate them for your own gain and expect to feel good.'

Mrs Heapey prepared to leave her seat.

Helpless and horrified, Tony looked on as Perfax slipped his hand down the side of the chair and pulled out a dart. With an expert aim, he shot the dart into Mrs Heapey and within seconds her body collapsed like a closing umbrella and she fell to the floor.

Scratching his leathery belly, Perfax sniggered, stepped over her and, disturbing the air with a final smelly blast, left the room.

Twenty-Two

The breathless whisperings of Bobbi beat in time to a flicking sensation on his cheek. Slowly he made out the slimy walls and the bright orange rug. The fluorescents were off, the room lit by moonlight alone.

'Wake up…Tony, open your eyes…' Her voice, low but insistent, buzzed in his ear.

'Your flace's blending into the ceiling. Uh…'

Slipping off through blurry, oily colours, Tony crashed into oblivion once more, his head pounding. Bobbi continued to flick his cheek until his eyes stayed open longer than five seconds.

'Your flace is s-swimming away in f-flour directions. Your eyes have flound your nose and your mouth's come back to be with your hair.'

His cheek began to sting.

'Aaoow!'

'Shushhh!' said Bobbi, 'sit up, I have to talk to you. Drink this, you might feel better.' Bobbi offered him some water, most of which he lost down the front of his shirt.

'Uh-huh, I've been out cold and just had the most humongously awful dream.'

'Never mind that now,' hissed Bobbi. 'C'mon.'

'Whattimeisit?'

'It's two in the morning.'

'W-which morning?'

Bobbi grabbed his collar. 'You need to leave now Tony, please. C'mon quick, get up!'

He lifted his arms and stretched his back. Someone had shoved his brain into a skull two sizes too small and his limbs had somehow morphed into concrete blocks.

I'm not sure that standing up's an option, never mind leaving in haste.

'Why aren't you coming?' he said, still lying on the sofa.

'I can't. I can't come with you.'

'Why not?'

'Shhshhhh,' said Bobbi, glancing over her shoulder, her face white and drained of calm.

'You're scared and worried Bobbi, why don't you answer my questions? What're you hiding?'

The questions hit the palm of Bobbi's raised hand.

He swung his legs onto the floor and the room began to melt. The walls ran into the carpet, which in turn ran into the walls.

'Try to stand up,' hissed Bobbi, holding out her hands, 'and lean on me.'

Staggering across the room they reached the corridor and using the bumpy stones that jutted out from the wall for support, managed to stumble to the front door. Bobbi opened it.

'Th-that's a t-tad cold.'

Finding his feet, he stepped over the threshold and out, where the night air sank its cold fangs further into his skin. Bobbi steadied him as he lurched forward, stopping to lean against a tree.

'We need to keep going,' she urged.

'Wait a minute, will you?' The chilly air was sharpening his senses.

The pair made eye contact just as the moon slipped out from behind a cloud, lighting up the landscape with an eerie glow. The raised wooden path rolled out in front of them like a narrow railway line, cutting its way through the slender saplings of the grove, the silver of their bark bright amongst the dusky shadows.

'I've forgotten my crash helmet,' said Tony. 'I'll have to go back, and don't say I can't because I have to, I've already been fined two weeks' pocket money for not wearing it and I'm not about to get fined again.'

Bobbi glared as Tony headed for the door, which hadn't closed properly, and pushing it open, he stumbled back along the stone corridor and into the dimness of the sitting room. Grabbing the helmet, he turned to leave, when a noise, a long whimpering moan, sawed through the air. Events from the previous evening began to drift back; thumping noises coming from upstairs, noises no one had explained.

Are these sounds coming from the same... THING as yesterday? There it is again, a moaning sound. It's more like a baby whimpering. A baby? That's a different noise. I wish I'd got a torch.

Pulling aside a curtain, he started to climb some stone steps, spiralling up towards the wailing. A single light bulb, dangling like a dead white rat suspended from its tail, hung at the end of the landing. A milky thin light seeped out, not quite reaching the cold dark patches that lurked, pitch black, in all corners. Wrestling his urge to spin and scoot, he flung open the nearest door and charged inside.

It's the b-bathroom.

The shower cubicle seemed to throb in the semi-darkness. White and muscular, it threatened to leap out, grab him and pull him into an alien plastic coffin. Stepping back, he tugged the door shut.

That made a bit of noise.

Shivering, he unscrunched his eyes and with wobbly legs, inched across the landing to another door. Trembling, he turned the handle and opened the door a crack. All was dark and silent. Slipping his head around the door, there, picked out in a pool of moonlight, was a small body in a bed. Creeping closer, he saw the body move.

It's Vicky.

Closing the door carefully, he stood quietly in the centre of the landing.

Another moany cry, and wait, that's Sherbet's voice.

'Nearly done now, swallow it up for Mummiedear.'

Here I am standing on a very strange landing in the middle of the night, cold, shivery and recovering from a whopper of a doping by some incredibly peculiar people. I am, without doubt, absolutely terrified. WHAT ON EARTH has possessed me to come up this creepy staircase in the middle of the night to seek out a semi-human moaning noise in somebody else's spooky house?

Paralysed, a thin film of sweat gathered at his hairline. A lump had lodged in his throat, so he tried breathing through his nose but immediately felt faint, his mouth dried up and his heart almost knocked him sideways with the punch of its thudding.

He tried to remain silent in the middle of the landing. A floorboard creaked.

Did I do that or is someone or something close by? I daren't turn around.

A slight movement in the air tickled the side of his head.

What's that? He batted the air by his ear. *Is someone creeping up behind me?* Squeezing his eyes shut, he waited, trying desperately to stop himself from screaming out.

Another whimper. Mrs Sherbet's talking to whatever it is.

'Just one more,' he could hear her say, 'just for me. No, swallow it I say, and don't bite. I said SWALLOW.'

Tony wiped the sweat from his forehead.

Calm, calm. Right, this has got to be THE door.

His hand hovered above the handle.

This is it, behind this door is an answer, or at least a clue to the questions in my letter. Has to be or why else would I be fighting a fear so enormous?

McGurney's calm encouragement bathed his shredded mind. 'I wouldn't leave you, if I didn't think you could manage.'

Well, I'm outside a bedroom door and I either open this door and find out a horrible truth or I open this door and find out a not-so-horrible truth, but either way I've got to open this door and find out.

Leaning forward, he turned the handle gently and pushed open the door.

Oh. My. Word.

Lit by a hundred candles, in a room full of cobwebs and big brown furniture, Mrs Sherbet spooned soup into the mouth of Prospect, who sat, strapped into a high chair, wearing a bib and dribbling down his front.

She's treating him as if he's her baby!

Stepping back, he turned and sped down the stairs and snatching up his crash helmet, let himself out into the pale, wintry night. As he left, a door opened and slammed behind him, followed by some heavy footsteps thudding down the stairs.

Bobbi was waiting outside. 'I am FREEZING, Tony, WHERE HAVE YOU BEEN?' Grabbing his arm, she pulled him away from the door.

Tony shuddered.

'You really don't want to know. Hey, where did you get that big trench coat and the scarf and mittens…?'

'C'mon,' said Bobbi, 'I want to see you out of here, it isn't safe.'

Tony's heart hammered. *I must get to the bottom of this wacky situation.*

'Are you staying here? Do you live here? For goodness sake, Bobbi, tell me.' Her face shone as white as bone in the moonlight, her eyes sad and tearful.

'You must have guessed,' she said, sighing. 'Mrs Sherbet and Prospect Sherbet are my parents, Appledown was my mother's name before she married, and this,' she gestured back to the black panelled door, 'is my home. I use Appledown because my mum's the headmistress and…'

'…And you don't want anyone to know. And Vicky, who is Vicky?'

Bobbi shrugged and turned away.

'Bobbi, who is she? What's she doing here?'

'Vicky has a purpose, it's not really anything to do with me,' said Bobbi, her voice trailing off.

Tony fell back against a tree.

'I don't trust you, Bobbi Appledown or Sherbet, or whatever your name is. I want to, really I do, but you have to help me out here, I have to understand.'

He scowled at Bobbi, only to see her features contort before him, her eyes widen, and her mouth form a silent scream.

'T-Tony quick, hide, get down! Get down!'

'No Bobbi, no more games. I'm not being taken in again.'

'Tony, I'm not joking, I'm being honest when I say I like you, I want to help, it's just…look behind you! Look!'

'Well it's great that you like me, that's for sure, but right now I think I'll just go back to my room and have a think.' He scuffed at the ground with his foot, glanced at Bobbi and turning to leave, walked straight into the sour stench and billowing flesh of the greeny-grey boy.

Twenty-Three

At two twenty-five on a cold Sunday morning, the knobbly, ginger-haired Tony Plumb and the lumpy, greeny-grey boy faced each other beneath an inky black sky, peppered with stars.

Surrounding them, the cage of silver saplings, their roots like elongated feet grabbed to anchor in the mud, their slender bodies grown tall for want of light.

Tony glimpsed Bobbi as she slipped into the undergrowth.

Both boys stood on the raised wooden pathway lit only by the full moon.

'I'm Perfax, why aren't you drugged?'

Perfax, the boy in the corridor and the boy in the dream. His skin's all lumpen on his face, like moist olive-coloured putty and he has no lips at all. That bulging colourless toad of a tongue is way too big for his mouth; and those nostrils, gigantic flaring holes, sucking in the air. But his eyes, ugh! Tiny green pebbles floating in briny jelly, staring at me, hollow and without feeling. Sooo scary. It's hard to find anything to like about him, that's for sure. Who the heck is this character?

The greeny-grey boy wore nothing but a school gown, that stuck to the smelly parts of his unwashed body.

'Er, hello Perfax, I woke up.'

'I see, so wakey wakey Tony Plummy, who has no mummy.'

Tony gulped. Perfax giggled.

'You, will be my friend now,' he said wagging his finger in Tony's face. 'You will come into my house and make friends with me.'

'Your house?' Tony's eyes rested for a moment on the black panelled door.

Was the dream true?

Engulfing him in a poisonous cloud, the stinking boy gripped Tony's arm. 'If you don't do this,' Perfax tittered, 'I will kill you.' The little eyes focussed. 'You'll be my special friend, or you'll become one of those stupid, useless friends of Ellodian, stuck here with nothing to do, your brain slowly rotting as you fester here, forever.'

Deeply creepy. So, the elderly 'friends' are trapped underground, having somehow failed a test set by Perfax. Charming. If he doesn't loosen his grip soon, I think my arm's going to drop off. What if that squelchy mud down there is bottomless, like quicksand? I could jump in and disappear right now, or better still, I could shove Perfax into the slime and escape.

Perfax sneered into Tony's face and dug his long dirty fingernails further into Tony's flesh.

I think blood's trickling down my arm. Blimey, he smells, it's like a blast from a sewer.

'You,' whined Perfax, 'will be my friend, which means you'll do all I say, when I say it. Now get inside my house and show me some of your fancy tricks, the ones that make you so nicey-nicey.'

'I'm going nowhere; my arm's gone dead, let me go!' Sweat rolled down Tony's spine. 'I haven't a clue what you mean by fancy tricks. I'm not nicey-nicey. Listen Perfax – I'm sorry but you've got the wrong guy.'

Perfax tightened his grip on Tony's arm and shook him like a rattle.

'If you want me to do as you say you need to let go of my arm.' *This is worth a shot.*

Excellent idea, this tactic worked for your mum. She was much smaller than your dad.

Shooting a fist up to Tony's neck and lunging forward, Perfax heaved Tony off the walkway, ramming his head hard against a sapling. A cold blue numbness grew in the middle of Tony's head. Perfax shoved his face up close.

'Don't you get smart with me you naught-ee orange giblet, or you'll never, ever, ever live to tell your pathetic little tale.'

Finding a foothold among some lumpy roots, Tony sprang forward, smashing his fists into Perfax, knocking him backwards off the walkway and thwack! into a tree trunk. Immobile for a second, Perfax closed his eyes.

Bobbi shouted. 'Now Tony, run!'

'What, and have this piece of ripe cheese come after me? No chance.'

Snorting clouds of cold air through his gaping nostrils and struggling onto some firm ground, Perfax ducked under the walkway and ran at Tony like a bull. Tony grabbed hold of a branch above his head and swinging his legs up, whacked Perfax in the face with his foot. Bobbi screamed as a sickening splat echoed around the wood.

Blood spilled from the gash on the greeny boy's chin. Perfax wiped his hand across it, casting his dull eyes down to study the glistening streak of scarlet on the pallor of his palm.

Just at that moment two things happened. Bobbi ran out of the copse in tears and it began to snow. Light, white, marshmallow flakes floated down, quickly forming a soft thick carpet that changed the light and muted sound. Violet flakes, iridescent almost, drifted silently, awash in the brightness of the moon.

The sticky red stream of blood dripped quickly from Perfax's chin, onto the fresh white ground.

All this blood!

Tony's shoulders dropped, and he hung his head, his conscience bitten by guilt.

This was the kind of fighting Mum and Dad did. Am I really like them? Could I be that bad?

Vaguely aware that Perfax was turning away, Tony looked up, but Perfax was only gaining enough momentum to spin around and WHAM! plant a heavy fist into the middle of his back, sending him face first into the snow-covered gravel.

'Aaarrrgghhh!'

'Ha! Eat dust you snivelling, ginger twiglet. Is your face shredded yet?'

Raising his head, Tony tasted sour blood on his tongue and spat out bits of lip. From the edge of his eye, something glinted in the trees close by. Stumbling forward, he seized hold of it. Perfax was close behind, about to make a grab when Tony swung around with a massive force and cracked Perfax full on with his yellow crash helmet.

Perfax went down. A lump the size of a tennis ball steadily gathered in the centre of his chest.

'Whaaaaa…! You idiot, you pimpled soggy carrot – I'm going to die! – Mummy, help me. Muummee!'

Perfax began to cry.

'It's not fair,' he whined. 'Where's Mummy? No one really loves me.' Snotty bubbles of blood dripped onto the surface of the snow, dotting the whiteness with small pink cups.

Is it safe to try to reason with him?

'I'm sorry Perfax, I don't want to hurt you, really I don't. I can see how it is, I know what it's like to feel like no one cares, but y'know I'm not smart,' he mumbled, 'I've never been smart and I'm lonely sometimes too....'

'Mummy c-come here!' Perfax didn't seem to be listening and instead beat the ground with his fists.

Tony remembered his dream.

'Tell me why you want me to be your friend?'

Perfax stopped beating for a moment, turned his head to the side and eyed Tony with a dull olive stare. Tony leaned on a tree and eyed him back.

I think he must be freezing, but behind all that dullness roars a massive furnace, blazing away. His energy is enormous. I can't let him hit me again though, my lip feels like it's been torn off.

Hauling himself up, Perfax lumbered over and stood beside him, big and blubbery, occasionally bouncing up on tiptoe before bouncing down again. The snot-streaked face and tiny olive eyes held an expression of immense, quiet hunger.

'I want you to be my friend because you're supposed to know how it's done. You're going to show me. Mummiedear has found me a girlfriend, my soul mate so-called. The bing to my bong, the white to my black, the top to my bottom or something... whatever...'

'Ah, you mean like parts of her that complement parts of you?'

'Oh! Some gushy-wushy, lovey-dovey rubbish like that...'

'But it's not rubbish, that's important stuff, it's how we get along...' said Tony, feeling himself warming to this likeable aspect of Perfax.

'No, it's absolute tosh and drivel. I want to marry Vicky and get my hands on her money, and I want my silly billy, plonker parents out of this school. I might even have to kill them, and THEN I can have it all for myself and rule everybody and be KING.'

'So, you are Mrs Sherbet's and Prospect's son and Bobbi...is...your...sister.'

'Umm, whatever,' trilled Perfax still bouncing, 'never mind the pin-head parents and the blister, cysty, sister, let's talk about me. The plan is easy-peasy really. I don't know why it's taking so long. Such a drag. When I get this place, I'll sell it. This is where you come in, my new bezzie friend.' Perfax leaned forward.

The dull olive eye raked over Tony with a scummy gleam.

'Mummiedear sometimes says things that are all right and she says you'll help me get what I want. Simple as that. You either become my friend and teach me how to be nicey-nicey and get my own way, or I kill you, it's your choice, dewdrop.'

'That's not friendship, that's domination. I don't fancy your idea much and anyway, if this is all true and you're the boss, why don't you just tell everyone what to do?'

Perfax turned away and then spun around, delivering a blow to Tony's head that knocked him out cold.

'DON'T,' Perfax screamed, 'set me questions I can't answer.'

Perfax grabbed hold of Tony's legs, dragging him up onto the wooden walkway and towards his mother's house.

Twenty-Four

Bump, bump, bump.

Aaoow, my head should not be bouncing off a stone floor.

Somewhere in the background Tony could make out a familiar voice.

'Oh, come on Prospect, you simpleton, we could let him have the money. Sign the papers.' It was Mrs Sherbet and she sounded annoyed. 'How is our beautiful young son going to grow into a wealthy, powerful, adult man if he isn't bunged a stash by his parents?'

'Bser…ser…'

'Prospect! I am asking you a question. I demand that you sign this house and the business over to Perfax. He is a darling boy and will do the best he can for our school, you know that he will.'

An ear-splitting smash, tailed by an avalanche of tinkly splinters, reached Tony's ears.

He's dragging me back into the Sherbet's sitting room. Play dead, play dead.

'What does the poor boy have to do to prove his worth? We had an independent examiner look at his grades.'

'You paid her dear.'

'I did NOT pay her...Shhhh! Was that the front door? He's here, Perfie's here. Get up Prospect, he might want to sit there. Go and make some tea.'

The sitting room door flew open so hard, it almost sprang from its housings.

'MUMMY,' a voice roared.

'PERFAX,' came the response, 'oh my precious perfect boy. How are we today?'

'You weren't there when this scuzzy scum bag hit me and asked me a difficult question.' Perfax let go of Tony whose limp and bleeding body fell to the floor.

'NO! I hope you hit him back my precious. Come and sit with Mummiedear on the sofa and tell me... oh...what's this?'

Tony lay slumped on the orange rug, barely conscious, his clothes torn, and his skin smeared with blood and mud.

'Er...should I take a look at him dear...I mean is he breathing...?'

'Stand back!' shouted Perfax, 'I think I am going to give him one more teensy-weensy chance to be my bestest ever friend, and if he doesn't obey me then I will...I will...'

'Now Perfax, let Mummiedear just check his pulse…'

'I said NO! You will not take a step nearer. SIT DOWN NOW!'

Sylvia Sherbet sat straight down, sucked in her cheeks, shoved her hands beneath her knees and subsided into silence. Prospect shuffled in from the kitchen with cups of tea for himself and his wife.

'Where's mine?' shrieked the boy.

'Er…um…yes…well, I'll get you some tea dabster, yes three-and-a-half sugars, yes.' Prospect put down his own tea and pattered over to give his wife her cup. Mrs Sherbet held out her hand and took the cup from her husband.

Excluded from his parents' exchange and having to wait a second or two for his demand to be met, Perfax began to scream and cry. Kicking Tony out of the way, he dropped onto his belly and pummelled the orange rug with his fists.

'Ah, poor Perfie,' cooed Mrs Sherbet, pushing her tea aside and pouring herself a whisky. 'Have you got a tummy ache?'

Tony's head throbbed from the kicking, but the blow had focussed his attention. Now fully awake, he inched further into the corner of the room like a snake who'd taken lessons from a crab.

Perfax bawled whilst his mother made random soothing noises from the side of her mouth. As if expecting her son's tantrum to last, Mrs Sherbet picked up a magazine, and with eyes as dark and blank as a shark's, flicked through the pages with one hand and ferreted in a box of cold pizza with the other. The fluorescent lights buzzed overhead and the heat in the room exaggerated all foul smells. Suddenly Perfax stopped, got to his feet and lumbered quickly out of the room towards the kitchen.

'Is Perfie getting himself something to eat? What a big boy! Does Perfie want Mummiedear to get it for him?'

Perfax stopped suddenly and returned to his mother's side. Wiping crumbs from her mouth she gazed adoringly at her son.

'Tomorrow I'm going to change the school colours,' he wheezed. 'I'm bored now with yellow, it's icky, so from tomorrow it will be green. It's your first job, Mummiedear. Get rid of those yellow helmets and bring in green ones. Say you'll do it.'

'PERFIE! You're so ecologically aware. What an environmentalist! Oh, my boy! I love you, I do love you.' Mrs Sherbet centred her flesh on the edge of the sofa, struggled to her feet, swooped on her son and kissed him on the mouth. Perfax folded and became quite floppy in her arms. Tony stared, his position slightly improved, having got two thirds of his body behind the sofa.

'My preshie, preshie Perfie.' She held him close.

'Say you'll do it,' wheedled her son.

'Do what, my grown-up boy, what do you want Mummiedear to do?' Perfax clamped his hand over his mother's face and pushed her back onto the sofa. Falling heavily, Mrs Sherbet sent cartons and drinks flying. The whisky glass spilled its contents, hit the floor and rolled towards Tony.

'GREEN HELMETS. SAY YOU'LL DO IT!' screamed Perfax.

'Perfie m-my darling b-boy, it m-may take time...I have to order n-new s-stock. It takes a while...'

Perfax ran into the kitchen, knocking over his father who was still on his way to make tea for his son, and came back with the bread knife. Seizing his mother by her crimson hair, he dragged her off the sofa.

'I don't want green because it's eco...whatever, I want green because it's the colour of SNOT.'

He waved the knife about, its long serrated blade glinting beneath the harsh lights.

Right under Tony's nose the whisky glass had come to a halt. As fast as an electric current, the combination of violence and booze connected and a similar time from childhood featuring his parents, flashed back.

Holey Jarlsberg, the smell of those drinks. I think I'm going to be sick.

Tony began to retch.

Dropping his mother quickly, Perfax hauled Tony out of his hiding place. Mrs Sherbet started to scream, Prospect turned in circles, and in a trice Perfax had Tony in an arm lock, the bread knife to his throat.

'This is where you die boy!' screamed Perfax.

'Sssh! Someone's here. There's someone at the door,' said Mrs Sherbet.

'You die, you die, you whingeing, ginger cringer.'

Mrs Sherbet clambered to her feet and headed for the door. Prospect pattered off upstairs.

'Hello,' the cheery voice of Mrs Heapey echoed down the hall. 'My, my Mrs Sherbet your ivy is growing exceptionally well for the time of year, the variegation is particularly impressive, I must come and take some cuttings. Is Perfax here? I have something I'd like him to see, something I've only just discovered, something NEW and unusual and very SPECIAL, something that nobody else has…It's a PRESENT for him…a TREAT FOR PERFAX, something I think HE'LL WANT.'

'Oooh no, Perfax is busy right now, he's just, well he's…He doesn't leave the house unless it's to go to his counselling appointment and only then when he's accompanied.'

Hearing news of a gift, Perfax dropped the knife, pushed Tony onto the floor and rolled like a cannon ball down the corridor.

'Give it to me now,' he trilled.

Mrs Heapey's voice grew quieter. 'This way Perfax,' she said.

'NO!' shouted Mrs Sherbet. 'No, he mustn't go, not without me or his father…er…wait…WAIT! MRS HEAPEY, I COMMAND YOU TO STOP. Oh my, it's muddy out here… my new leopard-skin slippers…too muddy. Mrs Heapey STOP NOW!'

'We won't be long,' replied the therapist, 'back soon.'

'PERFIE, COME BACK TO MUMMIEDEAR.' Perfax lumbered on and in response to his mother's pleas, he expressed a particularly throaty cackle, so loud that Tony could hear.

Twenty-Five

Slam! Thump, thump, thump.

That'll be Sherbet coming back down the corridor, and what's that rattling? Someone's trying to get in through the kitchen.

Mrs Sherbet's footsteps were at the sitting-room door when Tony saw Bobbi swiftly slip into the under-stairs cupboard.

I really think it's time to get out of here.

Spying his chance, he pitched into the kitchen, flinging himself out through the open window that Bobbi had just used to get in. Landing on a snowy bank, he let himself roll and roll and roll away.

Back at Ellodian, after a few bloody dabs with a towel, Tony ran to Mrs Heapey's consulting room. Opening her door, he saw relief sweep across her face.

'Tony,' she said.

'Mrs Heapey! You're OK? I mean, the dart...'

'The dart? You mean you ran here?'

'No, er – look, I haven't got an appointment…sorry I'm a bit muddy…'

'Never mind that now, sit down.' Her face seemed full of concern. Tony had never seen anyone take this kind of interest before. 'Are you OK?' she said.

Tony nodded. 'Sorry about last time.'

The therapist made a quick little movement with her hand.

'I know you must know something, in fact you probably know a lot about what's just happened at the Sherbet's,' said Tony.

Mrs Heapey pressed her lips together. 'Go on.'

'Well, I think you rescued me from that nightmare, probably with help from Bobbi.' His gaze was straight and direct. 'It was Perfax – I know you know him, I've seen him here, he tried to half kill me, no correction, nearly, really did kill me. Bobbi's back there now. I know Perfax left with you…' Tony searched her face for clues.

Mrs Heapey shifted slightly in her chair.

'A lot has happened,' she said 'and it sounds like dangerous stuff. Perhaps you need to tell me about it, and how you're managing what sounds like a nightmare.'

Tony noticed the frown across her forehead, understanding it to be a sign that Mrs Heapey was genuinely worried about him. Whatever she'd done with Perfax, Tony knew he could trust her.

He blew out a big deep breath and spread his hands out on his knees.

'There's so much,' he said.

'Well then, you had better begin.'

—∿∿—

'It's odd how all this has come about but I have to say it, and I have to say it now. Things have come together a bit, if you know what I mean.'

Mrs Heapey raised an eyebrow.

'Mum was as committed to Dad as she was to her own horrible habits.' Tony wiped some mud from his forehead with his sleeve. 'I've recognised this. Mrs Cubbage showed me how a mum might act, and Frank proved he knew how to be a dad. Both people have given me more in a few encounters than my parents did in my lifetime. I mean, they weren't bad people. My dad wasn't bad. I've changed my mind about that. He just didn't know what he was doing. I'm sorry they're dead, but they couldn't manage life. It's sad really, I think they did the best they could, but instead of helping each other, they just dragged each other down.'

Mrs Heapey gave a small nod.

'Mrs Sherbet's family is almost in a worse state than mine was, and I'm worried if something's not done someone might get killed.'

The turquoise eyes narrowed.

'Perfax,' said Tony, 'is spoilt and out of control. I can just see what's happening. It's like what happened to me. There he is, with a hopeless mum. She's doting and coo-chee-coo, but she's useless when it comes to helping him find out what's right and wrong, and what he can and cannot do. Perfax thinks he's the king of the planet. Honestly, he's bonkers.'

Tony glanced at Mrs Heapey who said, 'mmm.'

'I think another problem for the family is that Prospect behaves like such a wimp. D'you know why he calls everyone a dabster? It's to put himself down. The poor guy doesn't know what to do. He can't help Mrs Sherbet manage their boy and so the whole thing has just got out of hand. I honestly see Perfax's point of view, who wants a dad that's so soft he might as well not exist? Perfax isn't even enjoying all this so-called power, it just makes him miserable, he's desperate for a friend; it's so obvious. You once said to me that a boy must grow up and leave his mother. It's true, but the mum also needs to let go of the boy and maybe the dad should help her do this. Oh, I dunno, I guess Mrs Sherbet's worried she'll be lonely without her son. It's a nightmare.' Tony sighed, took a tissue from Mrs Heapey's box, dabbed some blood from his lip and carried on.

'Ethel and Frank are totally different to Sylvia and Prospect. I think it's because they are so together as a pair. I don't mean like they do everything together, they just seem to know where the other starts and ends, like separate people. Ethel knows where her own space ends and where Frank's space begins.'

'This is all very important Tony. You're definitely on to something, say a bit more.'

'Well, like Ethel has her feelings that fit with her job as a mum and Frank has his as a dad and they seem to, well, say nice things to each other.'

'As if they appreciate each other's role?'

'Yes, like that. The mole with a role!' Tony laughed. 'Aaow! My lip.' He dabbed it again.

'It's not like that with the Sherbets, they're all over the place. You'll never guess what I saw one night when I sneaked into their bedroom.'

Mrs Heapey spoke, 'I guess that must have been the point where you felt like you were treading in Perfax's shoes.'

'I don't know what you mean.'

A silence surrounded the pair and hung there like a water droplet gathering size at the end of a twig. Eventually the droplet fell.

'Well,' said Mrs Heapey, 'I don't know what you saw, and in a way, it doesn't matter. Being in a married couple's bedroom whilst they're doing something, seems to me to be the issue. It sounds like you think the problem for the Sherbets is that they don't know their roles, and that Perfax has been allowed to come between his mum and dad, taking on a role that doesn't help anyone. Now here you are, describing your decision to intrude into the bedroom of a married couple.'

Tony went white. 'Ah, but that's different,' he said.

'Is it?' asked Mrs Heapey. 'You've spoken of wanting your mum to leave your dad and be with you. Is it your role to come between your mum and dad? Do you think there might be similarities between you and Perfax?'

'Er, no, definitely not…'

'Hmm,' said Mrs Heapey. 'You have already suggested that Perfax has a very similar problem to yourself. He's found it difficult to separate from his mum too. In his case, perhaps it's because his mother can't let him go, and in your case because death prevented you from saying goodbye. Haven't both yourself and Perfax been trapped with very similar issues?'

Tony cogitated for a whole six minutes.

Mrs Heapey continued. 'I think as well, both yourself and Perfax have had dads that have let you down one way and another. Your dad didn't take the trouble to get to know you and perhaps Prospect doesn't know how to relate much to anyone, preferring to hide and give responsibility to others.'

Mrs Heapey's kind turquoise eyes twinkled.

'I see what you mean about the disappointing dad,' said Tony. 'Disinterested dad and weak dad might boil down to the same thing in terms of how they might come across. Then there's the mum thing. I guess when I said that I could leave my mum, because I now had you, I wasn't letting go of my mum at all was I? I guess I was replacing her with you. No wonder that didn't seem too much of a challenge!'

He chuckled.

'Oh yes! I've grieved for my mother, let me tell you how I did it. I just found myself a really nice therapist and wham! No more stress. Totally cool. Problem solved. So, I haven't really handled it at all have I? I've just shifted my feelings from her to you.'

Throwing the bloodied tissue into the waste bin, Tony sighed. 'That maybe explains why I felt there was a possibility that you drank too much and I could smell spicy smoke that wasn't really here at all. It was from my past, in my head as a memory, a memory I wanted to re-live with you. I'd made you my mum, but you're not her, you're different to her.'

Stay with it, don't give up.

Turning his head, he gazed up through a slim chink in the curtains to a pale lemon sky, dappled with soft grey cloud. A bird flicked past and he wished he were riding on its wing, away to another place.

Tony wiped a tear. 'Will you adopt me?' he asked, keeping his eyes on the strip of sky.

'No,' said Mrs Heapey.

Definitely give up on that one you dingbat — be realistic. Tony, you know this, but I might as well spell it out to you. To really love someone and be loved by someone you must know where they start and you end. You love the person as a separate person. At the moment you love the idea that Mrs Heapey should be an extension of yourself and could magically make everything all right for you. Grow up mate! She's a separate person! Know where your own space ends Tony.

'You've probably got about three or four children of your own anyway,' he said at last, facing her. 'Do you drink?' he said.

'Sometimes.'

Tony wrinkled his brow. 'What, like you're falling over and sick?'

'What do you think Tony?' she said calmly. 'Do I look like I drink so much that I fall over and am sick?' Her face was pleasant, open and inquiring.

Tony reddened. 'Er, probably not,' he said, smiling at his shoes.

'You haven't explained about the brandy bottle and in some ways now you don't need to. I think I know what sort of person you are.' He met her turquoise eyes.

Mrs Heapey nodded. Another silence settled in the room, but one more comfortable than the last.

'Frank's important to me,' said Tony 'and so is McGurney, they've both been good dads really. Did Perfax go to your home when you took him from Mrs Sherbet's?'

'Tell me what you think.'

'Well I just wondered if he'd met…?'

'You're wondering if he came to my house and met the husband and family you believe I have?'

Tony closed his eyes.

Don't give this back to me, I'm not hiding it for you. I thought we were having a bit of an emotional clear out? I don't think this should go back under wraps, do you? Why don't you answer the question?

'Hmm, I suppose I am,' said Tony. He stole a glimpse through the gap in the curtains again, but the internal mole tugged his awareness back into the room.

C'mon Tony, this is jealousy.

'I think I would be jealous if I knew that Perfax had met your family.'

'You sound like you're pretty clear that I have a family of my own,' said Mrs Heapey.

'Hmm,' said Tony. 'You probably have.'

Nice and steady Tony, nice and steady.

Thank you, mole.

'You're right, about what I said earlier, I did say that Mum should have left Dad and run away with me.'

Mrs Heapey nodded.

'I see what you're saying about their life together being theirs, but I think she should have got me to a better place, got herself healthy and everything, so she could take care of me and be my mum.'

Mrs Heapey nodded again, 'and maybe Dad might have done that too, if he could.'

'Yep. I do see now that Mum's relationship was, first off, with my dad. They were a pair together. Ethel Cubbage and Frank are a pair, like a couple I mean, y'know with an invisible boundary fence around them, marking them out as two people together. Perfax doesn't know if his parents have a boundary fence around them. He doesn't see his parents as a couple, in fact I don't think they see themselves as a couple!' Tony managed to chortle and Mrs Heapey's mouth twitched up at the side.

'I saw Mrs Sherbet take a tablet once at assembly. It was when I confronted her about the bolt that stuck out of the table leg.'

Mrs Heapey nodded. 'What do you think?'

'I wonder if she takes medication, I mean proper prescribed medication.' Tony frowned. 'Maybe she takes chill pills for her anxiety. She must be anxious with a son like Perfax. She's got a big job there.'

'That's a generous thought,' said Mrs Heapey. 'It sounds like you might be seeing things from her point of view.'

'Hmm,' said Tony. The session time was coming to an end.

'Tony, the work you have done so far in coming to terms with aspects of your parents, your relationships with them and others, and locating boundary fences, is very important and will help you with the next stage.'

'The next stage?'

'It's possible your memory will now begin to improve. This will be painful and difficult.'

'So speaks the supershrink.'

Being rude won't help you here. Manage your anxiety.

'Sorry, didn't mean that. I'm anxious.'

'See you next week, Tony,' said Mrs Heapey.

Twenty-Six

If I did it once, I can do it again, but how did I get out of Ellodian? It might be a case of mind over matter. If the House of Miniature Mail Boats is a portal, where letters come in, then maybe stuff goes out? What if there's a witchy-woo energy there that I can tap into and get out again?

Setting off to the House of Miniature Mailboats, Tony stumbled along the tufty bank.

This gown's blinkin' heavy, it might be easier down there.

Hopping off the grass, he landed on the crunchy gravel by the water's edge.

Splat.

'Yeuch!'

Why couldn't people pick up after their dogs? It's only a little poo, but it's all over my shoe.

Just by the side of his head, a dog yapped, a dog with a long coat, a curly tail and a squashed face.

'Here Pongee, here.'

'You're right. Pong – er, it deffo is!'

'What?'

'Your dog. I bet it was your dog that pooed here and…hang on, it's you, it's you!'

Wiping his shoe on some grass, Tony leapt up onto the bank and was about to pull off his crash helmet, when he realised he was wearing a jumper and jeans. A thought chariot rattled by carrying his gown and helmet. The image disappeared fast around a psychic corner.

'Mr Burrow, hello, it's me, Tony Plumb. Can I ask you some questions please?'

'Tony…er, Plumb is it, goodness me, where've you been? I've not seen you for, well, it must be nearly eight years. Pongee's an old boy now, it's the name of a Chinese silk by the way, and I'm getting on but I wouldn't forget that ginger mop of yours. Er, I must say though, sorry about your parents.'

'Yes! My parents, that's what I wanted to ask you about. When I met you, when I was little, you said you knew me, or you knew about me, well, what do you know? What do you know about my parents?'

'You might not want to hear it lad, it's not a lovely story.'

'I know that, but you see, I'm piecing stuff together. I know they struggled and got things wrong and I know about the waterfall, but not much about the waterfall.'

A cloudy veil fell across Mr Burrow's face.

'Aye, they were in a mess alright and they didn't take good care of you. Some around the estate say they weren't your real mum and dad; that they found you and brought you up as their own, but that's only what I heard.'

'Blimey.'

'Some say they stole you from somewhere, the hospital maybe. That's where Terry, your dad, if he was your dad, worked for a time, in the laundry. They'd lost their son Victor you see, snatched he was from outside the booze shop on the High Street. Daphne Jones had just popped in for supplies apparently, leaving Victor outside in his pram.'

Hang on, Bendy called me that…

'Jones? Their name was Jones, but how come I'm Plumb…?'

'Well I don't know lad, there was a rumour that you had a different name. Some said it was so they could disown you quick if there was a problem with the law, others said it was because they got a lot of sympathy and kindness as a couple who'd lost their son, so they said you were Daphne's nephew.'

'No kidding.'

'It was in the papers.'

'What was?'

'The story about your trip to the Lakes and the waterfall. Your so-called parents took you to the Lake District, a long drive it must have been from Evensham. At Pit Scar it was, near Kestwick. I only remember because Gladys and I went there for our honeymoon.'

'Go on.' Tony's stomach began to roll as a blurry image of thought chariots, a distant speck for now, thundered towards him. He snatched a deep breath.

'Well that was it. The papers said they jumped off Pit Scar Falls, a suicide pact or something. I'm sorry, Tony.'

'That fits with what I've uncovered, but it doesn't make sense, why would they…? Were they so upset and sad about losing Victor? Upset enough to commit suicide? And what about me?'

'I'm sorry, Tony.'

Tony couldn't get his breath.

'I need to stay, I need to know. I need…' But the thought chariots had blasted in, plucking him from Mr Burrow's side; whisking him away to another place in his mind, somewhere less disturbing.

Twenty-Seven

I'm getting pretty good at fishing for mail boats.

Tony peered into the tiny cabin. One letter. He opened it.

What? Amazing! I've been awarded a certificate, signed by Mrs Sherbet and countersigned by Prospect.

'Tony Plumb,' it said in big swirly letters, 'You are certified as successful, please go to Central Office where you can claim your award.' At the bottom of the letter in small pointy print it stated that the bearer could claim either a book token valued at five pounds or a raffle ticket that, if successful, would enable the ticket owner to:

a.   increase their chances of becoming a millionaire;
b.   win a holiday to the Bahamas by answering three easy questions;
c.   be entered into a prize draw where they stood to gain a large black car.

In a colourful band across the bottom of the page he read that two companies sponsored the award: 'Tippy Trashcan Tobacco and Cursed Kitchen Chemicals in Association with English Enlightenment,' it said.

What on earth am I reading?

He looked up. Standing by the main doorway was Bobbi, limp and pale and handing out green crash helmets. Although she was wearing one herself, he could see that she was crying.

Blood burned his face and clenching his fists, he walked over to the table where Bobbi stood. Surrounding her in the hallway were large packing cases, stacked with green crash helmets.

'What's funded this?' snapped Tony under his breath, 'a drugs cartel?'

He remembered the image of Perfax screaming at his mother to do his bidding. He reeled as the thought sunk in.

Of course, this weird stuff at Ellodian is all about Perfax. It's all about his enormous need to be king and the wielder of all power.

Tony, just think – if you were Perfax, wouldn't your search for power and position really, in truth, be about wanting to be loved and special to someone? You said yourself that he's desperate for a friend.

Er, thank you, Mole. I was trying to avoid any more comparisons between me and that boy.

...Well avoid if you wish but I'm only saying...

OK, OK, duly noted Mole.

Tony frowned and shoved his mind to focus.

All these daft, so-called traditions aren't old traditions handed down at all, this is the result of a spoilt boy's warped sense of humour and need to rule the world. The cruelty caused by these selfish, stupid schemes makes my stomach twist. Those monstrous crash helmets. Gaskin's helmet filling with water, almost drowning him; my head wedged between the table and the wall and Nelson's face gashed and bloody all because of Perfax's helmet rule. Just as bad's the total block on making proper contact; like face-to-face human contact. Everybody spaced out in their private world. What good is that? How is anybody going to get to know anybody else with their head encased in a helmet? How can anybody *make friends? It's totally bonkers; a safety device gone completely wrong.*

Tony kicked a tree stump.

So Ellodian exists as a tribute to Prospect, a failed man, Mrs Sherbet, an over-protective mother and a spoilt slug of a boy who thinks he's king of the world.

Mrs Heapey and Mole are right, my situation is similar to Perfax's but unlike Perfax I haven't had too much of my own way. Far from it. Despite my sometimes difficult...

Nightmare...

OK Mole, very difficult time with Mum and Dad and the horrors of Daisy Bank. I'd rather have had that than had Perfax's family any day. I s'ppose I've something to be grateful for.

The sorry image in front of him came back into sharp focus as the students and friends collected their new helmets.

They don't ask questions, they just follow orders.

Ask no questions…

*Forget that – RIGHT NOW. Instead **do** ask questions, ask lots of questions.*

Good one, Tony.

Tony returned to the moment and the scene before him. *There they go, all unknowingly programmed to do Perfax's bidding, carrying out the orders of a boy whose parents can't say 'No.'*

He could see now that Mrs Sherbet had prolonged the babying of her son, granting his every wish and whim so that he would never grow up and so never leave her. He recalled her recent screams 'PERFIE – COME BACK TO MUMMIEDEAR,' as Perfax left with Mrs Heapey.

No wonder Bobbi was crying. That's it! That's why she'd been so secretive and frightened. Bobbi's known all along that she can't get anywhere near close to her mum and dad because her brother takes all their attention and what's worse, Mrs Sherbet and Prospect allow it.

Hmm, I think Bobbi feels she doesn't really feature in that family; she's a sad, trapped young woman, who has no choice but to carry out her brother's bidding, issued via her mum.

He nodded to himself.

I can see now why Bobbi's been so horrible to Vicky; she can't stomach Vicky's part in the grand plan for Perfax, the favoured child. And look at her now.

One by one Bobbi dutifully took the new green helmets out of the packaging, waited while a student or a friend tried it on and then if it fitted, asked the person to sign a form on a clipboard, before beckoning the next person forward.

Enough!

Tony ran toward Bobbi. Bearing down at speed he grabbed hold of Bobbi's arm. A little cry escaped from her mouth as he firmly pushed her out of the way.

Tony glared at the crash helmets and Bobbi stepped further back, ushering others with her.

Tony struck.

Tipping over the table, he sent boxes flying and helmets bounced off in all directions. Then taking the helmets two at a time, he ran outside and started flinging them into the river. Some of them bobbed on the current, some of them sank without trace.

'C'mon, he's chucking helmets in the river!' shouted someone.

'He's totally lost it this time.'

'Sherbet's gonna flip.'

Panic levels escalated and screaming echoed through the corridors.

'Someone's knocked down a torch an' a fire's started in the hall!'

This news registered but Tony couldn't stop until every single helmet he could grab was in the river.

'Help me chuck these helmets!' yelled Tony.

Several eager students pounced on helmets.

Thwack! Someone tried to stop him. Aaoww! that was his sore arm. He glanced around quickly to see others strapping themselves into green helmets and shrieking for Mrs Sherbet as they ran from the hall.

'Watch it moron!'

'Don't push me!'

'No talking! Visors down!'

'Watch out idiot, that's another candle over. Yikes, it's got the tapestry by the door. It's going to catch fire. Move! Stop pushing. Let me out! Help!'

Students already in the river strode through the water, slipping and tumbling, aiming for the safety of the opposite bank.

'You're all being brainwashed,' shouted Tony, 'there're no worthwhile traditions at Ellodian. These are the arrangements of a dysfunctional family including a spoilt and disturbed child. You mustn't obey them. Listen to me. Do not obey. Try and get out now. Run and save yourselves.'

Gaskin scurried by and Tony saw that his furry chum didn't know who to obey.

'THE FIRE HAS TAKEN HOLD OF THE MAIN HALL.'

'Someone call the fire brigade.'

'Help me!' squeaked a young girl, who'd got herself stuck inside her helmet. She tugged, pushed and swung her head up and down, then staggered, tripped and fell into the flames.

'Let me through, let me through!' yelled Tony, reaching her just as her gown curled up in smoke, the flames licking her skin. Choking on the fumes, he caught her as she fainted, and bounding into the river plunged her completely under water. The rising hiss and stink engulfed him, but as he pulled her out, her eyes flickered. Dragging her back onto the bank, a breathless Bobbi materialised at his elbow.

'Let me help,' said Bobbi, taking hold of the singed girl's hand.

'Frankly…frankly…frankly,' but the elder stumbled in the melée and pitched onto the grass. Miss Woosey materialised from the mayhem, as white as a blank page, and helped Miss Frankly to her feet.

'Miss Frankly, shall I read some poetry? Would that help?'

Tony caught sight of Bobbi who was now slinging helmets into the water. The singed girl, her crash helmet now removed, rubbed her head and sobbed by the edge of the river.

A few discarded grey cloaks found their way into the river and floated downstream like lazy manta rays, as green and yellow helmets piled up around trees like ugly fungi.

'It's total chaos,' shouted Tony, running back through the main door with the hope of getting more people out. 'C'mon,' he grabbed hold of two choking students, 'this way, onto the bank, stay by the river.'

Above the din Tony could hear the distant maw-

mawing of fire engines as their lights flashed up and down the lane on the other side of the meadow.

There's only a dirt track across the fields and that's practically invisible from the road.

'They'll never reach us,' said Tony. 'They probably don't even know where Ellodian is, or worse, that it even exists.'

The sirens stopped.

'I've left my stuff in there. I'm going back in.'

'I need my asthma meds; can someone help me? They're inside my room, by my bed…'

'I have to get back in – get off idiot, you're on my gown…'

Like a shoal of frightened fish, several students quickly turned to re-enter the burning corridors.

'No, no! Come out,' Tony shouted. 'Come back to the river. Stay out of the building!'

With dirt-streaked faces and smelling of smoke, most students and friends began to throng the riverbank. A small brown figure in a checked cap appeared.

'Frank!'

'I'm here sir and I've got buckets. We're going to sluice out the corridors with river water.'

Tony felt sick.

Have I started this? What's the fire drill? Have we ever had a fire lecture? Then again, a notice could go up somewhere and no one might ever see it, never mind read it. I've been to every assembly but haven't heard Mrs

Sherbet mention a fire drill or even what to do in case of emergency. Where is Sherbet anyway?

The tall tutor with leaves stuck to his head appeared in his bathrobe and stood at the entrance. 'Silence everyone, visors down!'

Someone shoved him out of the way.

Frank helped the people with buckets to get organised in relay and water began to flood the corridors.

A thought chariot creaked off with Tony's guilt as he whirled around the scene. Charged now with adrenalin and powered by a sense that even though the fire was a dangerous, terrifying disaster, minute by minute something was clicking into place. The voices of active, enthusiastic people rang out.

'Hey, did you say your name was Derek? Over here – we need some more buckets. Watch it, there's a flaming missile, Ellodian's spitting 'em out. Duck!'

'Thanks. Yeah, I'm Derek, I've got some buckets, help me fill these.'

'Brilliant let's form a line; pass 'em along.'

***

'Help, I say, can someone give me a hand? This student's just jolly well fainted.'

'Move over, young lady, I used to be a nurse, help me take the helmet off. Careful. That's right.'

'My goodness me, he's as hot as hell's oven. I'll get a wet towel or something.'

'Wet his gown in the river, that's right, good. There we go. I think he's coming around.'

***

'Hello there, I'm Tina, how long have you been here? Hardly surprising, but I don't recognise you.'

'Ha ha! – Good one, funnily enough I don't know you either! About two years I think. I'm Gerry. Hello.'

***

'What's happened here today is nothing short of a miracle. I tell you, never in my six years at Ellodian did I ever think I'd see anything like this. It's amazing.'

'I agree, it doesn't seem possible and yet it's happening. Hello, I'm Ray, I think we sat next to each other at the Christmas lunch. Here, have a bucket, watch it, it's heavy.'

'Oh my! That was some lunch. Hi, I'm Lucille. This Tony guy's really rattled their cages. Pass me another. What did you think when he said…'

***

Like a buried, angry dragon, flames and noxious smoke poured from the portals of Ellodian, yet most people were smiling. There was a lightness, something gentle and easy in the atmosphere.

Tony scanned the scene. Prospect appeared from a portal.

'Prospect!' shouted Tony.

Prospect heard the voice and blinked.

'Over here...it's me, Tony...who else is in the building?' He remembered now, from years in care homes, that part of the fire drill was to have a roll call. Somewhere everybody's name should be on a list.

'Prospect! Get the roll call. Get the list of names. We need to see who's still in the building.' Tony pointed at a side door further along the bank. 'Please! You must know where it is.' Prospect disappeared into a side door as yet untouched by fire and seemed to be moving at a pace.

Bobbi sat the younger ones on the bank and set about making a list of names. Frank had found a hose and was creating a vacuum to suck water directly from the river. He waved at Tony.

'Fire's calming down over 'ere.'

Tony gave a thumbs up, and called to the last students to join the rest at the riverbank.

Silently, a figure materialised and shimmered briefly through the heat and smoke. Mrs Sherbet, her face ashen but composed, swept the scene with her flat, soulless eyes, before retreating into a dark corridor and away in the general direction of her house.

Twenty-Eight

It was half past six in the evening before it was safe to go back into the building. Amongst the dampness and quiet, the whole place reeked of smoke and charred timber. Mrs Heapey appeared.

Hang on, who's that?

Mrs Heapey was with a man. They were off to casualty with students who'd been hurt.

Hmm, that's her husband.

'Tom, could you help Lucinda and Gok? I've got Ali and Mae.'

Tom.

Watching Tom, Mrs Heapey and four children leave for the hospital, Tony forgot the fire and imagined they were off on a happy Heapey family holiday. The singed girl sat wrapped in a blanket on the back seat. It was the first time he'd seen Mrs Heapey close to a man, a man who was important to her.

They're obviously easy and relaxed. Hmm, there's a good, warm vibe between them.

A pang of something twanged in his chest. It burned and felt wriggly in an uncomfortable sort of way. *What's that feeling?*

Let me help. It's jealousy. Firstly, you wish you were part of that family and secondly you are now sure of Mrs Heapey's own special relationship, which doesn't include you. This doesn't mean that she doesn't like you or want to be your friend. C'mon mate you can handle it!

Tony took his mole's message on board and, strangely comforted, turned away from the scene. He would think about these things later. Right now, Sherbet was shouting into a loud hailer; calling a meeting in the assembly hall in two hours' time.

Above, a fire service helicopter circled, as the fire brigade made another attempt to reach Ellodian. The whirring blades of the machine got closer and a man leaned out of the cab, with a device not unlike Mrs Sherbet's loud hailer.

'We cannot reach you,' he said, 'do you have any casualties requiring an airlift to safety? I repeat, we cannot reach you...'

'We're fine,' said Mrs Sherbet with a blast. 'We'll sort ourselves out. No need to worry. The fire's extinguished. Cheerio.' She waved them goodbye.

Tired and wet, his nostrils stinging with the smell of smoke-singed wood, Tony harnessed a sudden surge of energy and flung himself into the air, waving and yelling.

'Come back,' he shouted to the pilot, 'come back.' But the helicopter turned and climbing higher, made its way over the meadow and out of sight.

Coughing and spluttering, Tony joined the crowd moving back into the building.

'Ouch! That was my foot!' said Tony. 'Aaoww!' A sharp jab in his back.

'You'll not last much longer. You'll get taken out, Ginge.'

'You evil boy. All this is your doing…'

He sighed.

My enemy count's rocketed into the stratosphere, 'specially with those who don't want change.

A couple of students patted his shoulder and then someone had the guts to whisper, 'Well done, totally cool, mate,' before disappearing back into the crowd.

Twenty-Nine

It was time for the meeting in the assembly hall. Tony took up position at the back of the hall, wearing a full school uniform he'd managed to salvage and piece together after the fire. Bobbi joined him in a smoky scented version of the same, complete with yellow helmet.

Something about her has changed, she's standing taller, her shoulders are straighter. She's not crying, and her eyes are alive and steely.

Acknowledging him with a brief nod, Bobbi gave his arm a serious squeeze. Fortunately, it wasn't the arm to which Perfax had applied his special flesh mashing tourniquet.

Gaskin came over and hovered quietly. The students in front of Bobbi and Tony turned around from time to time, glancing, whispering and nudging one another.

'How come those two are wearing their uniform?' said one.

'Dunno, wait and see,' came the reply.

Tony could see Frank by the door speaking to Mrs Heapey, now back from the hospital. Tony caught Frank's eye. Frank nodded. Mrs Heapey's face, as usual, gave nothing away.

She seems a bit out of place in the assembly hall.

I have already explained Tony, she doesn't live in her therapy room, she does have a life outside it.

Thank you, Mole, buzz off please.

A moment later Tom joined her and stood by her side.

Yep, they're close. Tony liked the look of Tom.

Frank Cubbage trotted over.

'Ow'd it all start like?'

'I think panic started the fire, but I think I started the panic.' Tony met Frank's tiny, shiny eyes.

'These crash helmets are ridiculous, and they're a danger. The thing is Mr Cubbage, Frank I mean, wearing crash helmets inside and every day like this, is bonkers and,' said Tony, clenching his fist, 'it's totally unsafe.'

'Rules is rules, and tradition's important,' said Frank, taking off his cap and folding it into the shape of a pasty.

'Frank, these helmets are sponsored by evil-doing companies with no morals and no respect. It's dangerous stuff we're dealing with. In fact, what happens here has got nothing to do with tradition or law. We're smack in the middle of a load of corruption. Ellodian is a good place, it works with nature, not against it, but nature sometimes makes people's heads break down, minds go wrong, and help is needed. It's a fearful, dreadful shame, but what's happened here with Perfax's demands, Mrs Sherbet's brand of authority and Prospect's position, has allowed Ellodian, the whole operation if you like, to be mismanaged. The corruption is everywhere.'

Frank's small eyes shot sideways.

'Are you going to speak out? Challenge 'em then, those in charge like?'

Looking directly ahead, Tony nodded.

'Aye, right then,' said Frank and unfolding his cap, put it back on. 'Right then,' he said, 'I'm with yer.' Frank patted Tony on the back.

'Me too,' said Gaskin, trembling.

Mrs Sherbet stood to address the assembly and an expectant hush descended.

What was that? She just made a gesture to Prospect. I reckon she wants him to play the school anthem, but look, he's not moving. She's actually pointing to the piano now and there's no way the little grey man is going to play 'Blue Suede Shoes'. This is not my imagination, Prospect is actually defying her.

No anthem materialised. Wrenching her eyes from her husband, Mrs Sherbet addressed the silent hall.

'We have had a fire,' she said, 'the first one I have ever had the misfortune to witness at Ellodian.' Her eyes fell upon Tony. Calmness lost, his cheeks reddened like the fire itself.

'You will have noticed that there are new helmets for you to wear. If you have managed to obtain your new issue then please, wear it as from now. If you had the misfortune to have your uniform tampered with and thrown into the river by ONE, MR TONY PLUMB, whom I will be speaking to IN MY OFFICE after this assembly, then you will have to wait three days for the next re-ordered batch to arrive.'

'He shouldn't have done it Miss,' shouted a small student at the front, strapped into a green crash helmet and clearly scared. Mrs Sherbet shifted her weight and her lips crinkled at the edges.

'Well I must say,' she said, slyly, 'I am pleased to see that our renegade has seen the sense to return to his full school uniform and hope that this indicates...'

Tony stood forward. 'I am wearing this crash helmet...' he undid the buckle at the side of his chin... 'so that I can take it off in front of you.'

Gasps rippled around the hall.

'Numpty.'

'Go on, Tony.'

'Plonker Plumb.'

'Wow, what's he sayin'? This is totally cool.'

'This,' said Tony, 'is to draw attention to a demonic force that has Ellodian in its grip.' A warm flicker grew in his chest.

'I'm sure I don't know what you mean,' said Mrs Sherbet. 'Everyone, dismiss.'

Three or four people began to move towards the door but hesitated, turning back to face Mrs Sherbet. The rest of the hall stood very still.

The headmistress tried again. 'Dismiss,' but the hall remained motionless.

Tony put his helmet on the floor by his feet. One or two other people still wearing them, did the same, including Bobbi.

'In case you didn't know,' said Tony, 'your son, Perfax plans to get rid of his parents; that's you Mrs Sherbet, as soon as he's worked out how to take care of himself without your help. This could be cool; achieving independence is a normal thing for a kid to do.'

Mrs Sherbet took a massive intake of breath and her eyes bulged.

'But what's not normal is that he's prepared to kill you to get his hands on Ellodian and the money he'll make. Which raises the question: just who or what is funding this institution? I'm sure I don't know, but I'm sure in time, I'll find out.'

A startled flash shot through the crowd. 'Meantime,' Tony continued, 'when Perfax has got hold of this building, he'll sell everything off to the highest bidder. This could be an ace move. Unfortunately, he's going to bully, beat and blackmail the students and friends of Ellodian into meeting his bonkers demands. This means that people will be pushed out before they're ready to go or face a miserable life of slavery.'

The room rocked and Mrs Sherbet turned magenta.

'Perfax sees himself as a grand and exceptionally important king, destined to rule everything and everybody without limits. From where I stand, Mrs

Sherbet, you only encourage him in these barmy ideas and so far, haven't found the strength…'

'….Or maturity,' someone whispered.

'…inside you to help him find better ways of growing up.'

'Get him out,' hissed Mrs Sherbet to Prospect.

'Listen. Everybody at Ellodian tries, like me, to help themselves. They don't want a pointless, useless life that means naff all, but the people I've met here think the rules and traditions of Ellodian are sacred. They truly believe they're handed down from the ancestors of Ellodian's medieval beginnings. Well, I can tell you, that's rubbish; cobblers, a complete lie.'

'Shut him up!' Mrs Sherbet snapped in Prospect's ear.

'You'll be telling us that St Elvis Presley wasn't a knight in Arthurian legend next,' said a middle-aged woman, squinting through her visor.

'Yeah,' said another, 'or that blue suede shoes have no significance in the making of the Roman Empire when it began in Hollywood in the 1800s.'

'Aaoow, that hurt.' *Oh, not again.*

Mean fingers pinched his arm. Tony stepped sideways, just as a boot poked out from the crowd and mashed his footprint.

'And what's more,' said Tony dodging a catapult's sailing missile, 'we don't actually have to wear these crash helmets, they stop us talking to each other.'

An elderly man with a walking stick spoke clearly from the back of the room, 'I suppose you think, Mr

Tony Plumb, that somewhere in the world people spend their whole lives without crash helmets and speak openly whenever they wish? To suggest we are being mismanaged indeed, what rot, I say. Have you no respect for your elders and betters? You, are a fool and must be deluded. There are limits you know, to what you can expect people to believe.'

Phwoorrr! That stink...

The stench flowed over the assembly and heads turned to see one Perfax Appledown Sherbet, wearing a bath towel and little else.

'Don't believe the dumbo Plumbo, Mummiedear, he's telling fibs and porkies.' People shifted their feet and a murmur rumbled around the hall like thunder in a boiling sky. The robed boy strode into the hall and pushing people aside, cut a path through the gathering.

Thudding heart, tingly skin, dry mouth. Stop it, stop it. Calm, calm.

Perfax lumbered over, wielding some sort of stick.

'I am the best. Got it? Superb, supreme, la crème de la crème, everybody knows that's me. I am your leader. Got it? My plans for Ellodian are superwuper-duper. For a start, adults won't exist. Anyone who's not a teen can stay, but only if they fry chips for breakfast and worship me, me, me and only me. Text books will be loo roll and chocolate will be everywhere, every day, all day, all year.'

Tony winced. *Hmm, with that diet he'll need all the loo roll he can find. Pity his brain won't be growing at the rate the library will be vanishing.*

'PERFIE, you don't mean that…'

'Shut up, you silly old bag,' spat her son.

Perfax raised the stick.

Hang on, that's a whip.

The crowd strained, someone squealed but no one moved.

Crack! Perfax's eyes gleamed. Tony's pale gingery arm split open with a shiny wound like a streak of raspberry jelly. Howling and holding his arm, Tony turned to Mrs Sherbet.

'You have got to help this boy to grow up.'

The whip flicked through the air again and several things happened at once.

McGurney flew down from the rafters where he'd been all along. Circling Perfax's head, he flapped his wings and the boy tottered. On cue, Tom Heapey and Frank rushed forward, felling Perfax. Tom neatly removed the whip from his grasp.

'Oohh,' cried Miss Woosey, 'this is horrible, so horrible.' She produced some smelling salts and fell backwards into the nearest chair. Bobbi went over to comfort her, Mrs Heapey left the room and Mrs Sherbet clambered down the steps from the stage and steamed toward her son at a great rate of knots.

'STOP!' came a new voice that cut through all the kerfuffle.

It was Prospect, standing on the stage, his hands on his hips addressing her directly: 'Sylvia, you must stop. Our boy needs help.' His voice was strong and incredibly clear.

His wife's head twisted around. 'Wha...?'

Absorbing Prospect's new stance, Mrs Sherbet deflated like a popped balloon and assumed a more approachable form.

Tony went over and took her hand. 'Your husband's right Mrs Sherbet, you must listen to him.'

Tony looked at Prospect and Prospect met his gaze. With that, Mrs Sherbet began to bawl and Miss Woosey, about to offer the headmistress a small lace handkerchief, placed it instead on Tony's wounded arm. Tony dug in his pocket and offered Mrs Sherbet one of Gaskin's crumpled swans.

Mrs Sherbet's eyes were fixed on Perfax. 'MY BABEEE!' she wailed.

'He's no longer a baby, Sylvia,' said Prospect, 'he's a grown-up lad. Come on now, you can't baby him forever, let him go.'

At this Perfax sat up and stared at his parents with a lot of interest.

Prospect turned to some of the staff, who watched immobile, speechless and struggling to think.

'Can someone call for a doctor?'

Mrs Heapey re-entered at this moment and said she had just done that very thing.

'MUMMY!' screamed Perfax and the whole room jumped.

'PERFIE!' screamed Mrs Sherbet, tears spilling over her cheeks like bouncing beads from a broken necklace.

Perfax scrambled to his feet and Mrs Sherbet tottered toward her son.

Instantly Prospect was between them.

'NO!' he said, 'Perfax, go and sit on that chair over there with Mrs Heapey. Sylvia, you must try to give Perfax some space.' He took hold of her plump hand.

For a second, Prospect seemed taller than his wife. Mrs Sherbet looked up at him. Her eyes glistened with tears but also with curiosity and a faint sparkle of hope.

Bobbi came and sat on a chair beside her brother, who seemed relaxed for the first time and smiled. He had a nice smile, sort of goofy and quite cute. Sylvia shuffled toward her children but kept Bobbi and Prospect between herself and her son. Mrs Heapey moved away. The family Sherbet sat together, an awkward arrangement, but they were together.

The assembly broke up, and chattering, people left the room.

A small pale hand waved and calling him over, Mrs Heapey drew him to one side.

'Tony I'd like to offer you an extra session or two, there's a lot going on for you right now. What do you think?'

Tony nodded.

Thirty

Tony flopped into his chair opposite Mrs Heapey.

'I get it, I totally get it.'

'Ah! Right, go on.'

'Ready?'

'Ready.'

'I can now deffo move on to the next stage, as you call it, because I've shed the need to be my mum's special boy and compete with my dad to be the best guy. Even though in reality he wasn't such a good guy at all, I still wanted to prove I was better than him. I feel bad that I put him down so much. He was just a man with problems, much like most of us, but I'm not excusing his drug taking, deffo not, or Mum's either. So now, after that scene in the dining hall, I feel I'm well, sort of me, if y'like and not someone who's fighting to be better than a dope-headed boozer dad he didn't really know.'

'Mmm, sounds like there's more.'

'There is. Remember I told you I'd got out? Well, I think I'm nutty, right, but not all the time, sometimes I'm not nutty, I mean not mad, and when that little window of mental wellness opens up. I'm kind of back in the real world.'

Is Mrs Heapey crying?

'Are you OK?'

'Yes,' said Mrs Heapey blowing her nose.

'I think there's a lot you could tell me, like straight off, but I think I've got to do it for myself, like I'm doing. Is that right?'

Mrs Heapey nodded.

'Good. You probably know better than I do that it's difficult for me to be sure if I'm well, or if I'm not. I don't know if I'm well right now, or if we're in a room courtesy of the NHS, social services or some charity, or if I'm at Ellodian in a psycho scene. The curtains and blinds are always drawn, for privacy, I understand that, but where am I? I mean, where am I right now? I know I came here to my session along a corridor, but even now I can't remember if it was an underground tunnel or a carpeted hallway.'

'Go on,' said Mrs Heapey.

'Well in a way it's pointless looking through the window, because I don't know what's real. I mean I know you're real. You are real, aren't you?'

Tony stared at Mrs Heapey who smiled.

'You seem all right, even if I might not be.'

'What?'

'Real.'

'Look, I'm just going to carry on and work this out. The test is, can I read the stuff that's in my rucksack? They're letters. I got hold of them once when I was out. Last time I tried to read them, it was like watching worms dance.'

'Do you want to read the stuff in your rucksack here and now, with me? We could make sense of it together.'

Tony pulled out the photocopied papers he'd lifted from Ellie's desk.

'Don't tell me how you got hold of this right now,' said Mrs Heapey, 'just read as much as you want to and stop when you're ready.'

McGurney's words floated into Tony's mind.

I wouldn't leave you if I didn't think you could manage.

'I guess you wouldn't say I should read it, if you didn't think I was well enough.'

'Sometimes thinking about how well we are mentally, is scarier than experiencing our emotional selves in action.'

'I think that means just do it.'

'If you feel ready.'

'Right. One's a letter written by Bendy, dated about a month ago, and the other is some sort of report from October 5th, 1965. Hey – that was when I was five. OK. Here goes. I'll read the report first. At the top, underlined it says: "Tony Plumb, question mark, Jones." Y'know, Mr Burrow told me about the Jones thing, he said rumour is that Terry and Daphne aren't my real parents and, get this, I was stolen or taken maybe, from the hospital. That's where Terry worked apparently.'

Tony looked at Mrs Heapey, who looked back.

'Then it says: "DOB: unknown. Youngster says he's five and a bit and that his name is Plumb." Did I really say I was five and a bit?'

'You were only five Tony.'

'Hmm… "Any distinguishing features: Ginger hair. Former address: 81, Glubbins Road, Evensham. No known relatives."

Then it says:

"12.45pm – Call taken from Kestwick Social Services Children's Department referring youngster Tony Plumb to Evensham S.S.C.D. Transfer from Kestwick arranged.

"Youngster Plumb found with two adults Daphne and Terry Jones, now deceased, at Pit Scar Falls Kestwick, last Tuesday. Home address apparently located in Mrs D. Jones's handbag.

"Emergency Case Conference planned for Monday.

"Psychological report requested.

"Entry made in Missing Children's file.

"Evensham Police notified and aware. Spoke to Inspector Hector Blunt who stated that local news coverage from Kestwick will be rolled out nationally by Evensham police, with a Special Police Bulletin asking for relatives or anyone with information to come forward. Nothing to report to date. Inspector Blunt stated he would be speaking with the local paper the Evensham Chronicle and making an appeal.

"Please Note: The Jones's son Victor Elvis Jones is still missing see case E326745."

This raises more questions than it answers,' said Tony staring at the other piece of paper on his lap, 'and there's more.'

'Tony how do you feel about reading more right now? There's quite a lot to think about and to make sense of it properly might take more time. What about waiting a while, maybe think about what you've just read?'

'No, I'm cool, the thought chariots are tied up in the compound and I'm cool. I'm going to read some more.'

'If you wish.'

'Aah! This other one's to you Mrs Heapey. It says it's a referral. So, Bendy referred me to you, did she?'

'Yes, we spoke on the phone sometime before that letter was written.'

'Yes, it says, sorry for the delay in writing. Bendy says I'm bright and deserve more than routine placements would offer. Hmm. It says the psychologist's report states I have episodes of psychosis, right, well, I know that now, and what else? Let me see, what does this mean? Something unpronounceable, O-ee-di-pus, what's that?'

'Important theory. It's pronounced "Ee-di-puss". Greek myth. Boy falls in love with his mother and kills his father, both acts undertaken without boy knowing it's his mum and dad.'

'Mmm…and that's something to do with me?'

'Maybe. These assessments are a guide for me, but what's important for you, is what you make of our relationship.'

Tony paused for a moment, his head on one side.

'Do you think I wanted to kill Terry?'

'No, not really, but you did want to fight and compete with him.'

'True,' said Tony. 'It also says Terry and Daphne Jones had substance misuse problems and were grieving for their lost boy, Victor, who was apparently snatched from his pram as a baby. Mr Burrow told me that, that must be true.'

'Tony, isn't that enough for now?'

'S'ppose. The rest just says thanks and get in touch if you need any more information, but I guess you know that.'

'I'm thinking, Tony, that it might also be useful to meet up with the doctor from Evensham before you decide what you want to do next. I can arrange that for you.' Mrs Heapey smiled calmly. 'You could meet the doctor here. We might invite Bendy Leggett and I could be present at that meeting as well, if you like?'

Tony slid off his chair and pushing the papers back into his rucksack, made for the door.

'Session over,' he said.

Thirty-One

'Mornings are the worst times,' said Tony to a black beetle as it made its way along a tree root. He swung his legs out of bed and wondered if the heaviness inside his head would ever lift. He pulled some ivy away from the tap and splashed his face.

Silly crash helmet, stupid gown; still, rather than cause any more kerfuffle, maybe I'd better put them back on for now.

Why? Don't you have the courage to stand by what you said?

I do, Mole, and I will. It's just that we have to choose our battles and fighting on the corridor about helmets is one I'll save for later. At the moment, something tells me I've got a bigger boil to burst.

He opened his bedroom door.

Another day in Madsville I guess. Whoa! Carpet squares, that means... Tony quickly checked his head... *yup, it's gone, no helmet, things are looking up. Where am*

I? I reckon if my healthy mind is working to help with my mad bits, then I should be in Evensham library. Yes – I am!

'Hello,' he said to a woman who appeared to be coated in dust, 'Could you help me please? I'm looking for the local papers, back copies, y'know, archives. Could you…'

'Over there,' she said, extending a bony finger.

I know now it was 1965 and I was five when the waterfall thing happened. Bendy's report was October so that's likely when they died. He pulled down a cardboard box from a line of labelled boxes on the shelf.

Tony be careful. This is fresh territory, are you emotionally prepared?

Thank you, Mole, I'm fine.

1974, January – March.

'Wrong box. Aha, here are the sixties.' Tony pulled out another cardboard box.

'Ssssh! No talking,' said someone from behind a bookcase.

Tony dropped the box. Screwing up his eyes he tapped his head.

Phew, just hair. Thought chariots? Nope. Garaged for the day, or at least the moment.

A red bus went past the window.

'It's fine, I'm fine.'

'Ssshh!'

'Sorry.'

'Ssshh!'

He gathered the papers together and got them roughly into shape. The top edition had big capital letters on the front page.

'EVENSHAM HOSPITAL IN CUTBACK CALAMITY'

Tony scanned the headline. *What date is this? April 1960, that's my birthday month. If Mr Burrow and the rumours about me being taken were right, should I be searching for news about hospitals as well?*

Tony chewed his lip. *Hmm. What had Mr Burrow said?*

'Some say they stole you from somewhere, the hospital maybe...'

If Terry took me from the hospital when I was just born, this article might be worth a look...

EVENSHAM HOSPITAL
IN CUTBACK CALAMITY
By reporter Peter Packer

Evensham Hospital is to be the subject of an investigation, it can be revealed.

Why so many staff have left their posts and have not been replaced was a question that officials at the top could not answer.

Mr James F, 67, of Evensham-on-Sea now convalescing at home after recently spending a week in Evensham Hospital, made the following comment:

'Well, the hot meals were a bit chilly, the wards were all a bit grubby, spiders were undisturbed, and we couldn't get hold of a bed pan for love nor money.

'Beds were on wheels and parked on corridors. Sometimes, a bed that should be on one ward ended up being shoved on to another. It was terrible. Why, only last week when I was an inmate meself, I overheard staff on ward 1B say they had 10 patients and staff on 2A say they had 9, or was it the other way around? Anyway, when I counted there's only space for 8 beds on each ward so they're surely heading for a cutback calamity. It stands to reason, anything could happen. The wrong operation, the wrong ward, the wrong patient – anything.'

Tony tapped the page with his finger. If the hospital was that chaotic, then Mr James F, whoever he was, was right – anything could happen.

Tony took a deep breath and read the article again.

'…The wrong operation, the wrong ward, the wrong patient…'

The wrong baby?

A tear gathered. Determined, he reached up to the shelf for another box, but paused when he found his other hand still hovering over Mr James F's words.

The laundry. Mr Burrow said Terry worked in the laundry. How would I end up in the laundry? There's still a lot I don't know, let alone understand.

A wet splodge slipped onto his cheek.

Sad, I feel so sad, funny but it's a whole lot better than feeling mentally run over by vicious chariots with spiky wheels and an agenda of their own.

Another big tear plopped onto the newspaper. Drying it off with his sleeve he traced his finger further along the row of boxes.

1963

1964

1965 Now where's the October box? Here it is October-December.

Tony found the paper.

It was on page two.

BOY SPARED AS PARENTS JUMP IN POSSIBLE DOUBLE SUICIDE PACT

Police in squad cars gathered at Pit Scar Falls near Kestwick yesterday evening, when local artist, Alice Seymour aged 24, reported an incident involving the deaths of two adults from Evensham. Ms Seymour made the following statement at 9.05am today:

'I saw a family, two adults and a young boy standing at the top of the falls. I'm local but I've never been here before. I approached them and asked if this was Pit Scar Falls. It all happened so quickly; I couldn't see everything. I don't think I realised they were so close to the edge but suddenly they'd gone and the boy, Tony, was on his own. I sat him down and ran to get help at the information centre.'

Pit Scar Falls attracts many visitors on account of the waterfall, which is said to be the longest drop of water within a hundred miles. The drop terminates in a deep, rocky pool where police divers pulled the bodies of Terry Jones aged 29 and Daphne Jones aged 27, from the water yesterday at approximately 5.15pm.

Inspector Hector Blunt from Evensham police is assisting Kestwick police with their enquiries, but to date it is thought that there are no suspicious circumstances surrounding the deaths and that it is likely to be considered a tragic accident.

When asked Inspector Blunt made the following statement:

'We are appealing for witnesses to come forward to add to information we already have. It's possible they merely slipped but forensics are not ruling out suicide. Investigations of exactly what happened here, are currently at an early stage.'

'Blimey that's me,' said Tony out loud as he took in the blurry image of himself. 'And that's them!' Next to the photo of himself was a picture of Terry and Daphne.

Tony sat down on a step stool and the sweats returned.

Keeping a tight hold of the paper, he rubbed his hands on his jeans and peered closely at the image. Terry wore a pale blue tee shirt and had a narrow face with a mouth set in a straight line. It was difficult to see his eyes, as light reflected off his spectacles. He'd combed his wiry brown hair back from his face and wore something shiny around his neck. By his side Daphne smiled, her shoulder length blonde hair held to the side of her face with little hair slides shaped like bows. He studied her face carefully. She was smiling, true, but her eyes were cast down and, in a way, she looked sort of sad, as if she might need a sleep. The couple sat in a bar, both with a drink in one hand and a cigarette in the other. Tony noticed Terry's tattooed arms but couldn't make out much of the design.

Beneath the photo it said:

'Daphne and Terry Jones pictured last year at Evensham's Bar-a-Go-Go.'

The images swam as his tears came thick and fast. He remembered them, he remembered.

He was pushing open the back door, the television hummed, and that funny smell drifted throughout the house, the thin wisps of smoke that took his mum and dad to another place. He was standing in the hall; both his parents were on the other side of the door and he knew they were in the middle of one of their funny conversations.

'He's a lovely boy, don't get me wrong,' he'd heard Mum say. 'It's just that I find myself thinking of Victor all the time and sometimes I just can't stop crying. The other day I tried to make him some sandwiches to take with him, y'know when he goes out to play, but I just couldn't do it. I found a box to put them in and I found a bit of bread, but in the end, it just seemed too much. I couldn't do it. Poor mite I hope he found some food somewhere.'

'Kids today they're resourceful, that's what they are; a dab hand at looking after themselves.' Dad had said. Tony remembered Mum saying something about feeling useless and wanting Victor.

'Oh, for Gawd's sake shut up will yer!' said Dad.

'Shut up yourself!' Mum was screaming now. A glass smashed against the wall.

The little door under the stairs, yes, that's where I'd go and hide. Inside was Dad's old scooter gear. The helmet, muffling their screaming, safe now, safe…

The images collided with a flash back of the house, a scrappy end to a neat and handsome terrace. There it stood, uncared for and crumbly, with weeds thriving in the patch of garden that led down to the river.

Almost as if he was watching a film, another memory crashed into his mind.

'Mummy, Daddy look!' He'd been playing outside by the riverbank and now stood before them, the small furry creature held gently in his cupped hands.

'Look, Mummy look…' Eventually, first Mum and then Dad swung their heads to see what he held in his hand.

'He's got a mouse or summat,' his dad had said. Mum didn't respond, she didn't usually, especially when she was smoking. Neither of them seemed interested. Tony remembered standing there for ages.

'Look, look…'

'Whatever it is go and throw it in the bin,' said Mum at last. Her heavy eyes closed and her head rolled back.

'Can I help?' A middle-aged woman stood by his side, her hand on his shoulder.

His parents and their sitting room slipped away, his vision clearing enough to make out a blurry figure with a kindly face leaning over him.

'My nose is dribbling, an' my throat aches and everything hurts. Everything hurts. Ev-erything hurts. E-ver-ry-thing hurts!'

KER – R – UNCHH! The thought chariots smashed through the glass wall of the library, heading straight for him. Images of Daphne and Terry swirled around him.

'It's ov-over-whelming, th-the stink o-of their d-dr…and it's d-deafening.'

'What's deafening you, dear?' said the woman, sitting down beside him and offering a tissue.

'The water, it's the loud water. The sound of rushing water.'

Thirty-Two

Mrs Heapey's eyes remained reassuringly turquoise.

'You need to know Mrs Heapey, that I'm truly pooped.'

'I hope the rest time has helped.'

'Rest time? Huh, is that what it's called? I've had a blip, but before that I was well and I went out again. I found out some more stuff, a photograph of Mum and Dad in a bar and a woman who was actually at the waterfall when it happened. It's awesome, but I'm sad, really sad.'

'I understand this is hard Tony.'

'What's good is the sadder I feel, the less mad I am, well I think I am. Does that make sense?'

'Yes Tony, it does. Feelings can be painful. Sometimes it's just too hard to bear them. You are understanding your feelings more, which I think means it's easier for you to tolerate and manage them.'

'Is that when I go mad then, when I can't manage the feelings?'

Mrs Heapey moved her head a little.

'I think soon I'll be ready to meet with Ms Seymour, the artist who was at the waterfall.'

'Tony, do you want someone to come with you?'

'Are you offering?'

'Well…'

'I don't think that would be a good idea because boundaries or messed up boundaries are what got me into this nightmare in the first place; kids in charge, mums and dads taking orders – the wrong parents in the right place, the real parents, who knows where. Victor missing, not with his parents, well unless they're all together in heaven. Me in Madsville one minute and in the real world the next. Don't get me wrong Madsville's helped, but only because I can look back and understand when I'm well, I mean with your help. Perfax needed help to straighten out his boundaries. The Cubbages, a family definitely sorted with their boundaries, to me they are how a family should be. So…'

'So…?'

'I'm going on my own. You're my therapist, not my mum or travelling companion, and any support I need, I'll talk about in my next session? Deal?'

'Deal,' said Mrs Heapey.

Tony opened the door.

'Do you know where Kestwick is?'

'Map,' said Mrs Heapey.

'Map,' said Tony and closing the door, turned to find himself on Evensham High Street.

Thirty-Three

Let's see, enough from my pocket money for a cuppa and a flapjack, but that's it.

Heading for the bookstore, he stopped by the queue at the till.

'Excuse me, do you know where Kestwick is?'

'That's in The Lakes I think, Moira, Kestwick? Isn't that in The Lakes? Yeah, the Lake District, up north, off the M6.'

'Thank you.'

Tony found the map section at the back of the shop. Aware of the staff at the till, he hid behind some shelves and kneeling down, spread the map out on the floor. It stopped at the bottom around Manchester, but he could see Kestwick, further up, just off the motorway. He folded it up. On the back of the map was a picture of the United Kingdom, divided into squares. Each square was numbered and, *coolio*, each number corresponded with a separate map.

'Right so I need to try and memorise this one and this one. At least I've got some idea now. I'll be OK once I get a lift.'

He put the maps back on the shelf, walked out into the early spring sunshine, hoisted his rucksack up onto his back and following the big blue signs, headed for the motorway.

—∿∿—

'It's more like a shed than a truck stop café,' said Tony to himself, as he walked into the massive car park of 'Meals on Fire'. The lorries towered above him, their wheels about his height. The lorries were parked at an angle and in rows.

Fred Mercer Haulage, Birmingham. Nope.

G W McKenner Corporate Catering Systems, Aberdeen. Maybe, but I wouldn't know where to jump out.

Arnold Bickerish Ltd. Wholegrains Nelson, Burnley and Colne. Those places don't ring any bells, but if this truck's going north and there're sacks in the back, it could be a comfy ride. Hmm, it's smaller than the rest, I can j-just about r-reach...

Pulling at some nylon rope holding down a canvas cover, he peered into the back of the truck.

'Oi! Ginger. What'r'y'doin?'

'Er...'

'You thinkin' of stowin' away by any chance, or are you out to nick stuff?'

'Er...N-no not nicking anything.'

'Where y'tryin' t'get to then?'

The man was red faced and beefy, he wore a blue and white check lumberjack shirt and a baseball cap that said 'New York' above the peak.

'I'm trying to get to Kestwick, it's just off the motorway.'

'Aye, I know where Kestwick is.' The man cast a glance over Tony as he re-tied the canvas cover. 'You seem a bit young to be travelin' alone.'

Tony's eyes slid sideways and he shrugged his shoulders.

'C'mon, I'll give yer a lift, but mind, I want something in return.'

The man began to walk towards to a bright green and blue lorry that said 'Blatts of Butterthwaite for Bubbling Baths and Showers' on its side. An image of a shower cubicle showed a penguin with a loofah under its wing about to climb in. The shower looked OK. Tony followed. The man disappeared around the huge nose of the lorry with its window sized headlights and snarling grille. Tony hung back until the passenger cab door popped open. A comfy-looking seat awaited at the top of a metal ladder.

'You comin' or not?'

'You said you wanted something in return?'

A newspaper landed with a thud at his feet.

'I'm one clue away from a fifty-quid prize. Can I find the answer? Can I nelly.'

Tony picked up the paper and climbing the steps, pushed it back onto the seat.

'I'll have a go.'

'Get in Ginger, we got just over four hours.'

—◦◦◦—

'Thanks a lot Mister, and thanks for the crisps.'
Tony climbed down the steps.

'Well, thanks to you buddy, for the answer. Never
woulda' got that funny name from 'Mythic Scandal
for Greek Boy and his Parents', but listen mate, not
everybody's as nice as me, you get me?'

—◦◦◦—

Kestwick was smaller than Evensham with one main
street, a church and a bridge over a river.

Tony opened the palm of his left hand to check the
name.

Alice Seymour, artist

The felt tip pen had smudged in a crease where he'd
written 'artist.'

Where will I find artists?

The church clock chimed three times.

Why not try there?

The church was made of stone, blackened with age
and had posters in the porch.

*OK, a bring and buy sale scheduled for next week,
a bible reading class every Monday and what's this? The
bell replacement fund has reached one hundred and five*

pounds. Good for them, but nothing here for me. Right, let's try the high street.

At the opposite end of the street to the church Tony found the information centre.

'Hello,' he said to a woman at the desk, who smiled. 'I'm looking for an artist, she's from here I think. Alice Seymour, do y'know where I can find her?'

'Has she got an exhibition?'

'Dunno.'

'Details of all the current local exhibitions are on that board over there and I think there are some business contact cards pinned up as well. Failing that you could try the telephone directory.' She smiled again.

Tony nodded. The board yielded nothing and although there was an A L Seemer in the local directory, he didn't think that was worth spending his last few pence on.

So, back onto the main street.

A woman in a long, patterned skirt with a scarf around her head walked past.

What did an artist look like? He spotted a bench and sat down.

'You here for your holidays?' said a wavery voice to his left. Tony turned to see an elderly man in a flat cap, shirt and tie.

'No, just here for the day, well I think for the day.'

'I expect your parents are out and about, are they?'

'Well, yes and no. Er, I wonder if you can help me?'

228

The man sat up straighter. 'I like to be of help where I can. In the war I was stationed at…ah well, I'm sure you don't want to hear about that. What can I do for you?'

'I'm trying to find someone, her name's Alice Seymour.'

'Alice Seymour, God rest her soul. You'll find her in between Mr Collins, who was the best butcher Kestwick ever had and Mrs Olive Partridge née Cobb, by the water butt that collects from the transept, nearest the gate.'

'From the train set?'

'No, the transept, you know, part of the church.'

'What, you mean she's working in the church?'

'No young man, I mean Alice Seymour is dead.'

Thirty-Four

Dusk crept across the sky, as Tony wandered into the Kestwick Convenience Store.

'Cheesychomp?' said a girl with very pale skin and plaited hair. In her hands she held a tray of yellow things, arranged in rows.

'Hmm. Thank you, Hilary,' said Tony reading her badge.

'Have another, oh you have, well, have another. Yes, no, no, just carry on. I've got to give all these away by seven.'

'What happens at seven?'

'My dad picks me up.'

Tony nodded and took the last Cheesychomp. 'Do you live in Kestwick?'

'Mmm, well, just outside, do you?'

'No, I'm from Evensham, further south. I need to get back there.'

'When?'

'Soon as. The person I came to see is, er – not here.'

'Oh?'

'She's died.'

'Oh.' The girl's pale skin coloured slightly, and she looked down at the empty tray.

'No. I mean no need to…sorry,' said Tony. 'I didn't know her, she's not a relative or anything.'

'Oh. OK.'

'Anyway, thanks for the cheesy chips.'

'Cheesychomps.'

'Yep, those. See you.'

'See you.'

Tony started the walk back to the slip road where the lorry driver had dropped him off.

Too bad she died. I've come to a big full stop.

Sitting for a moment on a bench beneath a street lamp, he considered the questions. *What happened to your mum and dad? That means how did they die? I know they went over the falls, but I don't know why. Alice Seymour might have helped me answer that.*

Tony gazed out into the darkness beyond the bright patches of light and suddenly, the question got bigger, much bigger.

Hang on, if Daphne and Terry weren't my real parents and they stole me from the hospital, then somewhere, I've got another *set of parents; a biological set of parents and the question might also apply to them. The question 'What happened to your parents?' also means what happened to my* **real** *parents!*

*They're out there — but **where?***

Discs of light shot by as he gazed into the traffic.

They're still around — somewhere.

His knee began to bob up and down at a rapid rate. The thought of parents, real alive parents, was almost too much to contemplate. Steadied by the list of questions, Tony returned to question three.

Who, am I? Hmm, I think I'm a bit clearer about that one.

A car pulled up, the window went down, and a man said:

'You're the young man going to Evensham aren't you?'

'Yes, I am,' said Tony, seeing Hilary's pale face smiling up at him.

'Want a lift to the motorway?'

Tony climbed in the back.

'Who's picking you up?' Hilary's dad drove across the bridge and parked in the car park by a sign that said 'South Bound Traffic'. The car park was empty, and the garage was closed.

'Umm…I was going to cadge a lift.'

'What!'

'Dad, could he have the spare room and go back tomorrow?' The girl spun around and pushed her head between the seats to smile at Tony and whisper 'Is that OK with you?'

Tony nodded.

'Well, yes I suppose he could,' said Hilary's dad. 'What about your parents, sorry, what's your name?'

'Tony Plumb and my parents are dead.' *Not strictly a lie.* 'I'm at a boarding place outside Evensham. It's called Ellodian and that's where I'm heading.'

'I'm John, by the way. Do the staff at Ellodian know you're here?'

'Yes,' said Tony remembering his conversation with Mrs Heapey. *Not a lie, they kind of know.*

'You sure? How come they'd let you go on this trip without an escort or without a ticket?'

'It's complicated,' said Tony quietly, 'and I am quite grown up.'

'Dad, don't…'

'Hills, Tony might be in trouble.'

Hilary stuck her head between the seats again. 'Tony, are you in trouble?'

'No.'

'There you are.'

'Hmm,' said Hilary's dad, 'I think we'd better help you get to where you're going.'

———ᕦᕤ———

The spare room was small and seemed odd. It was all pale blue and everything matched. No ivy. There was just one bed in it, which wasn't made of metal. No bunk beds with 'Property of Evensham Social Services' written in green paint on the headboard. Swirly wallpaper covered the walls.

No sign of any tree roots and, coolio, a carpet.

Tony lay in bed and stared at the ceiling. His head felt like a sponge, a saturated sponge. So much to think about…A memory drifted in, a memory of when he'd been alone in a bedroom in the Lake District before, many years before.

It must have been when I was five. The waterfall thing.

Tony closed his eyes. The images came back, clear and vivid.

'C'mon Tony up you get,' said Dad, 'we're off for a picnic.'

Mum was there, staring at him blankly. Something was wrong. He remembered wishing he could be with the friendly grey bird with the cherry red tail, the one they'd seen recently at the zoo. Dad was red faced and annoyed, Mum distant and pale, both smelling of something funny. The memory brought on a shiver and his limbs ached.

'Will there be sandwiches?' he'd asked.

'Yes,' said Terry.

'…and cake?'

'Yes.'

They'd walked for ages, stopping people to ask directions. When they'd left the town behind, they came to an open grassy bit.

Mum and Dad weren't wearing the right clothes, just cotton things and sandals. Crazy! It was October. Totally embarrassing now, but back then it just seemed normal. Funny how Mum and Dad were walking in silence.

Tony twitched when he remembered the gushing sound of water ahead. As the path opened out, they'd entered a clearing and stood at the top of the first waterfall he'd ever seen. It was huge.

He gasped. Now, as then, it was scary and amazing at the same time and now, as then, his heart thudded and he snatched at breath.

Calm, calm.

Clinging on to the pale blue quilt, a vision of crashing water and spray flying up from the rocks, reappeared in his mind and the thunderous noise filled his ears. He remembered taking a step towards the drop and peering over the edge. Cold air rushed up to meet him and a great swirling pool of froth and bubbles swished around, a long, long way down.

Whoa, please don't frighten me, please, whatever you are.

The distant silhouette of a ragged, spectral figure leapt into a big, black thought chariot and sparks shot from the wheels. The rumble began. Getting louder. And louder.

''Night Tony!' sang Hilary's voice outside his door.

The thought chariot crashed and a wheel doinged off, bouncing out of view.

''Night, er, Hilary.'

'It's better if I take you back into Kestwick,' said John at breakfast. 'If you're going by train there might be one that goes straight through or you can get the coach, at least to Birmingham. Could someone from Ellodian pick you up?'

Hilary leaned over and whispered something in her dad's ear.

'Good point Hills. Have you got enough money for your ticket?'

'Er…well.' Tony looked at the toast crumbs. 'No, that's why I was trying to cadge a lift.'

'Hmm I see, a bit dangerous that,' said John. 'Well, I'll tell you what, here's a fiver, it'll get you to Evensham and buy you some lunch, but I expect you to pay me back. You have our address. Any time in the next year will do, but it's not a gift.'

'Cool. Thanks a lot, er J-John.'

'Good,' said John.

'Good,' said Hilary and winked.

Tony smiled.

Back in Kestwick he bought a train ticket straight through to Evensham.

'When does the train leave?' he asked the ticket seller.

'15.23, platform two.'

'What, twenty-three minutes past three?'

'This i'n't London laddie, there's no direct trains to Evensham most days. Today you're lucky 'cos there is. At 15.23. Next.'

Tony swung his rucksack on his back and wondered what to do with the next five hours. Wandering back onto the high street he saw the church steeple. *Might as well go and read gravestones, there's not much else to do.*

Here lies Alice B. Seymour
Loving Wife and Mother
May she rest in Peace
February 27th, 1970

So, she's only been dead three years.

The clock struck ten.

Tony sat down on the grass, leaning back on the stone marking the grave. The trees looked like trees and not doorways and the grass looked like grass. The wind rustled through both.

I like being above ground; no helmet, no Ellodian, no bonkers staff this time and only real sadness to keep me company. If McGurney were here, I'd ask if these were normal thoughts. They feel like normal thoughts. Does this mean I'm a saddo? He let out a sigh. *I don't think I'm a saddo but I can sometimes be sad. It's a relief really, to feel sad about sad things.*

He chewed on a stalk of grass.

I wonder where Terry and Daphne are buried? I wonder if my real parents are alive? To answer the question: Who are you? I think I do know who I am. I'm a young man trying to piece my past together. I'm not a big, super cool hero, or a lad fighting for power over his dad and I'm not a mummy's boy either. I'm sometimes not so well, I know that, but I've got support.

An image of Mrs Heapey floated in his mind's eye.

Mrs Heapey. S'ppose I'm quite lucky to have had her helping me.

...and the other questions you're trying to answer?

Thank you, Mole. All right, so how come I've been in care since I was five? I think I was left in care without fostering because no one wanted a bonkers kid. A kid lost in Madsville.

He balled up his fist and stuck it in his eye socket.

That leaves the third and final one, the one it seems I'll never, ever be able to answer.

A light wind swished through the tops of the trees and made a murmuring sound.

'Hello,' said a voice from behind.

For a tiny moment, Tony thought he was going to turn and see a mud-walled corridor and feel the weight of a helmet on his head.

'H-hello,' he said and scrambled to his feet.

The woman was about thirty and wore a long black woolly coat, a stripy hat and green boots. In one hand she held a bunch of daffodils that hadn't yet opened and in the other a plastic bag.

Whoa! she's got a knife in that plastic bag and her hands are flecked with blood.

'Er, I'm going,' said Tony.

'It's alright, I'm just doing some weeding.'

Glancing back, Tony saw that it wasn't a knife but a shiny trowel, and picking up his bag he walked on, through the gravestones and back up towards the church.

Rooks caw caw-ed around the steeple and Tony found a seat by a yew tree. He swung his feet up on the bench and was about to lie down, when he saw the woman again in the distance. She bent down over a grave and then stepped sideways and crouched, her face looking towards him. That face bending down, looking at him, those particular movements registered deep within his mind, and somewhere a memory began to take shape. He watched her stand and turn, and then she took off her hat. Long purply hair fell around her shoulders.

Tony ran to the grave. The woman was digging at Alice Seymour's grave.

'Did you know her?' Tony almost shouted as he pointed at the gravestone.

'Yes, of course I knew her.'

'How, how?'

'She's my mother.'

───❧───

He stared into the woman's hazel eyes. Yes, they were flecked with orangey slivers, unusual, but instantly recognisable.

It's her.

'How do you do,' she pulled off a gardening glove and offered him her blood-spotted hand. 'I'm Alice Seymour, named after my mum.'

'H-hello, I'm Tony Plumb, named after some people…'

Alice dropped her glove and her hand flew up to her mouth.

'You're *the boy*.'

Tony nodded. Alice picked up the trowel and the weeds and put them into the plastic bag. The daffodil buds lay by the grave.

'Let me get some water.' Alice stood for a moment, silently acknowledging her mother's resting place. Then, picking up a jam jar from the grave, walked slowly to the water butt. It took an age for her to return to place the daffodils in the jar and set them gently by her mother's stone.

'I suppose you want to talk to me?' she said quietly.

'Y-yes please, I've come from Evensham, I've been searching for you.'

Alice seemed to be breathing hard. 'C'mon' she said, 'I'll put the kettle on.'

Thirty-Five

Small and painted white, Alice Seymour's cottage had one downstairs room. Between the sofa and the kitchen, tubes of paint, a roll of material and piles of newspaper littered the floor. The place smelled of turpentine.

Tony noticed a cloth with some red paint on it.

'I thought you had blood on your hands,' he said as she handed him coffee.

'Oh, my gracious. Please! No! I hope to goodness not.' Alice Seymour snatched up a cloth and rubbed hard at her fingers. Five minutes later she was still rubbing.

'You look a bit frazzled,' said Tony.

'Do the police know you're here, or your doctor? Does your GP know you're talking to me?'

'My therapist knows.'

'Your therapist, right. Well, I've known this day would come,' said Alice.

'How do you mean?'

Alice put down the cloth, sat down and pulled a cushion onto her knee.

'I knew you'd find me and I've often wondered what I'd say to you when you did.'

'So, you've been thinking about this since…?'

Alice nodded. 'Um…this might be a bit awkward.' She paused. Tony held his breath. Finally, she spoke. 'Can you tell me what you remember?'

'Yes, I s'ppose I could…I was…'

Alice patted the air and shook her head. 'You don't have to tell me, it's not my business anyway. Maybe I should just tell you what I know.' Alice hugged the cushion, her coffee cup untouched. 'It's been years, you were a little boy.'

'Yes, it was eight years ago. I can remember bits,' he said.

'You are still quite young, I don't want to cause any…'

'It's all right. I'm thirteen and I need to know what happened at the waterfall. I know I was there with my mum and dad. It was today you see, when I saw you crouching at the grave, I remembered you. I was five when I last saw you crouching down and looking at me. Please tell me what happened, I've got support and I want to know. It's cool. You can tell me. Please.'

Alice blinked.

'Part of me thought, if Tony Plumb comes to see me I'll say I don't remember anything and wait till you went away.'

'Why would you say that?'

'Good question.'

'But you do know something, you remember, don't you? Are you, will you, I mean are you prepared to…?'

Alice's eyelids flickered.

Tony waited. *Is she going to tell me or not?*
Hang in there Tony.

The cushion on Alice's knee rapidly changed shape as she kneaded away.

Trying not to sigh, Tony shoved back his fringe.

Alice fidgeted. 'Perhaps if I went for a walk? I might relax a bit.'

His watch told him it was nearly twelve noon.

Alice stood and reached for her woolly coat.

'I'll come with you,' said Tony.

'No please, just give me a minute or two. I'll come back. I've thought about this and thought about it and now you're here, it just seems so sudden.'

A tear sprang. 'Please come back and tell me, I need to move on, I need to know.'

Alice nodded.

'Where shall I wait for you?' said Tony.

'The bench, the one by the yew tree.'

———※———

The church clock struck one and Alice was nowhere. Trying not to stare relentlessly at the gate, Tony followed the flight of the rooks as they circled the steeple and hid in the trees.

They might be parrots, McGurney's family. They've come over from Africa to find me and they're here to keep me company.

One large rook sat on a branch, away from the rest and fixed him with its eye.

Just a minute, that isn't a rook...

The leaves began to rustle and murmur.

'*Yes, you're quite right...*'

He stood and walked toward the bird, which took off and landed in another tree. Its feathers gleamed, giving off a silvery sheen and Tony could swear he'd spotted a streak of red. Squinting up into the tree he missed his step and stumbled on the gravel path. The crunchiness underfoot disturbed the air. Distant rumbling? Thought chariot rumbling? The bird fluttered and hopped onto a branch further away.

McGurney...? The bird cocked its head.

'McGurney? Is that you? I questioned Ellodian, like you said I should...I...'

Clunk.

The metal gate to the churchyard swung open and coming up the path was Alice.

'Tony, I'm sorry to keep you waiting, that was terrible of me. I'm ready to tell you now. It's only fair.'

Tony exhaled and looked up. The bird was a rook and the air around hung still and silent.

'Are you alright Tony?'

'Yes, thank you, I am.'

'Can we talk at the train station please? It's just my train's due in a couple of hours.'

'Yes of course.' Alice hoisted her brightly coloured patchwork bag further up onto her shoulder and the pair set off to the station.

The café was almost empty.

'Let me buy you a drink,' said Alice.

'Thanks, just tea.'

'Two teas please.'

Alice put the tray on the table and sat down.

'Ready?' said Tony.

'Yes,' Alice stirred her tea. 'W-well, I couldn't see everything, I said that to the police at the time. I'd been walking and done about two miles. It was the first time I'd been there and as I came to a clearing, at the top of the falls, I wanted to check out where I was. I saw a couple, a man and a woman and figured they were on their own,' Alice sipped her tea, 'then I saw they had a little boy with them, about school age with,' she nodded at Tony, 'ginger hair.'

'How did I look...I mean, was I having a good time?' Tony touched his chest. *Calm down.*

Alice shook her head.

'No, you were terrified. I'll not forget...Hang on Tony, is this all right? Are you absolutely sure you want me to go on?'

'Please, don't spare anything.'

'It's very awkward for me because I told the police what I saw, and they said, well there's no point repeating that now, because they're dead.' Her chocolate, orange eyes were wet as she shifted her gaze to look directly at him. 'No point repeating it, it'll only cause problems. That's what they said.'

Tony put down his cup, for fear of spilling his tea.

Alice pulled a tissue out of her bag.

'G-go on.'

'I thought they were just sight-seeing, so I walked toward them and said – "is this Pit Scar Falls?"' Alice put her paint-dotted hand to her chest and inhaled. 'But before they fell…before that…before…'

'Yes, w-what…?'

Alice looked at him.

'They each held your hands and were counting one, two, three. They were swinging you over the drop. Tony, they were going to throw you off.'

Thirty-Six

He found a seat in a corner at the back of the train.

Swinging you over, swinging you over, going to throw you, going to throw you.

The motion of the train repeated the words as it rattled south. Being sick at Kestwick station had helped.

One two three, one two three, swinging you over, swinging you over, going to throw you, going to throw you.

Going to throw you off.

Tony held his head in his hands. The thought chariots jostled for position and he strained to keep them under control.

Thank the holey cheese, they're not breaking free, I'm actually holding them back! My mental barricades seem to be holding up. Yippee!

Tony this is hardly the time for yippee. You should slow down and maybe speak to Mrs Heapey. There's a lot to think about. This is big stuff...aaarrrghhh!

Thank you, Mole, no I mean it, thanks, but I'm not

stopping now. There's something positive in what Alice Seymour said; she said they fell. That means they didn't want to die and that's good. I think it's time to get off.

The train sighed to a stop. Slamming the train door, Tony headed toward Evensham High Street.

'Bar-a-Go-Go' was covered in graffiti and squashed at the end of an alley of old blackened bricks. Hearing a noise, Tony squinted down a tiny passage that opened out into a yard. A man with damp stains under his arms tipped crates of empty bottles into a skip.

'Excuse me, I'd like to speak to the manager or m-maybe the barman?'

The man glanced up. He had a natty haircut and wore pointed shoes.

'What's it about?'

'I was hoping to ask a question…you see my parents used to come here, but they're dead now.'

'Oh yeah – well I'm sorry kid, but they didn't die in here.'

'No, I didn't mean that.'

The man trapped a rolling wine bottle with his foot and tossed it into the skip. The crunch of glass smashing on metal echoed down the passage.

'I'm the manager, what do you want to know?'

'Er – well, Daphne and Terry Plumb – er – no I mean Jones, they were my parents – well sort of, anyway, I'm trying to find someone who knew them, anyone who might be able to tell me a bit about them. I was very young you see, when they died and…'

The man cleared his throat. 'I get you. Were you adopted?'

'You could say that.'

'I was adopted too.'

'Oh?'

'I've only worked here four years, but there's someone here who might help. It's a tough one. I tried to track my parents down when I was a teenager.'

The man stood staring into space.

'What happened?'

He shook his head. 'No deal, I got nowhere.'

'I'm sorry.'

'Well maybe it's better this way, who knows?'

'You said there was someone here who might…?'

'Mrs Hanks, Teresa the cleaner, try her, she'll be in the bar. She's been here years and knows pretty much all there is to know about everybody. If you're asked, tell them Johnno said it was kosher. Go through this way.'

The rooms smelled of stale smoke, sour beer and pine disinfectant. Considering the place was so small from the outside, the inside was huge with corridors snaking off to staircases and rooms within rooms. Tony saw a sign that said 'Public Bar'.

An elderly woman in a green and black spotty overall was collecting glasses and putting them on the bar.

'Right that's me Josie, I'm off now.'

Mrs Hanks shed her overall and hung it up under the stairs.

249

Tony spied his chance and approached. Mrs Hanks had very small, silvery eyes.

'Well, I'm on my way to Bingo lad but I'll give you ten minutes; sit here.' She stared at an alcove.

'So, who wants to know?'

'I'm a relative, well a sort of relative, I was…' Mrs Hanks didn't seem to be listening.

'Daphne and Terry Jones, you say? I remember them like it was yesterday and I remember that tragedy, awful it was. You must have seen it in the papers?' Her head swung around and her eyes, like silver pin-heads, caught him in her gaze.

'Go on,' said Tony, perching on a chair. 'I was very young at the time, so…'

'Oh well, very young, were you? So, you won't know how bad some people can be.'

Tony bit his lip and mumbled that there were a lot of good people too, but Mrs Hanks pressed on, oblivious.

'Not enough love in the world that's the problem, except for those closest to God and I'm meaning one in particular.'

'You s-seem very well informed.'

A small ripple moved across her shoulders, as she pulled in her chin and settled in her seat.

'Not everyone's privileged you know,' she said.

'Mmm?'

The silver eyes remained fixed. *Did her tongue just flick out?*

'Well there is something, but I can't say, no I can't say, it wouldn't do.'

The pin-heads rounded on him and her white stare burned his cheeks.

'You see I could help you by sending you to Father Andrew, but he's gone, God bless him. He was a good man, a good man.' Mrs Hanks gathered together the beer mats which were scattered on the table and began to build a little steeple.

Was Mrs Hanks bribe-able?

Tony's fingers located the pound left over from the money Hilary's dad had given him.

'But then again, Father Andrew was sworn to oath, so he wouldn't tell you either. It's private, you see, what happens in the confessional is private. No one must know. Only the privileged. Father Andrew wouldn't say anything…'

His chest tightening, Tony scrunched his hand into a fist and shoved the money deeper into his pocket.

I don't think money's going to shift her.

Stay with it.

'Daphne and Terry said something in church, at confession?'

'Terry? That's a laugh, I never saw Terry in the church and when I'm not here I'm there, doing the flowers sometimes but cleaning mostly, it gets dusty beneath the pews and round the organ; sliding around on the floor, so many little bits and pieces to clean, the bibles, the cushions and prayer books on the floor. But

Terry in church, ha! You're having a laugh you are.'

'So, it was Daphne, Daphne said something to Father Andrew, is that it?'

Tipping her head to one side, Mrs Hanks added an extension to the steeple. Her eyes stayed fixed and a little cold smile coiled around her mouth.

'Oh, I couldn't say, really I couldn't. You see what's said in the confessional is strictly confidential. Father Andrew would never say, no never. Anyway, I must be off…'

'Well in that case Mrs Hanks,'

You smarmy sna…

No – no – don't say that…

'…you must have overheard, and what's more if you were snooping around the confession box, you would be prying and betraying whatever trust the Father had in you.'

Mrs Hanks's tiny eyes rounded larger than before and a hiss escaped her lips.

'You cheeky…'

'You'd better tell me.'

'Or else…?'

'Well, the church's still there, with a Father hearing confession and at the moment you still have your job…'

'You wouldn't say anything…?'

'Well no – if you tell me what you know and don't dangle half-truths to make me squirm.'

The cleaner's eyes bulged, and her scaly hand wavered around her mouth.

'You promise…?'

'I'll not tell anyone – but I need to know, so…'

Mrs Hanks glanced around the empty bar. Extending her endless neck, her head recoiled and then she darted up close.

'It was Daphne, she said she'd lost her son Victor and that she'd adopted a boy, unofficial like. Said she got him from the hospital; a mix up. A likely tale if you ask me. She wailed away in that confessional box like a banshee, that's how I could hear. She said Terry's plan was to end the misery of not knowing what happened to Victor, by ending the life of the adopted boy. By killing him, that's what she meant. Oh, it's disgraceful! Ruddy murder-makers, but Father Andrew wouldn't tell and neither did I. I hinted loudly enough to the police at the time, but they didn't listen. Didn't want to know. I couldn't say anything specific, out of loyalty to Father Andrew.'

Mrs Hanks crossed herself. 'He'll forgive me for telling you because he'll see the awkward position you've put me in, you varmint. Father Andrew bless him, took this to his grave. I don't think he believed they'd carry it out, I mean she was a drinker and weak, but Father Andrew didn't know Terry. He was no good that one. After Daphne's confession, Father Andrew was desperate, I could tell, but he wouldn't speak out. "We all have our burden to carry Mrs Hanks," that's what he said to me. Didn't know for one moment, I'spect, that I knew exactly what he meant, but I did, I did.' Mrs Hanks dabbed her eyes with the back of her hand. 'It was our little secret, but *he* never knew *that I knew...*'

Tony stared at her.

'So, you see lad, they were planning to put Victor to rest, through ending the life of this adopted boy they'd got their hands on. His funeral would be Victor's funeral as it were. Daphne Jones was crying, saying "Terry wants an end to all the not knowing," that's what she said. Madness if you ask me, madness.'

I think I'm about to throw up.

Me too...

Tony pulled a serviette out from between the tomato sauce and the mustard, but Mrs Hanks whisked it from his fingers to dab her eyes. The beer mat steeple fell over.

Calm, calm.

'What were they like, Daphne and Terry?'

'Drinkers and muddle-headed half-lives, they fell off some waterfall in the end.' Mrs Hanks, stood up.

And the rest. Breathe, breathe.

'You've made me late for Bingo. Now, you keep your trap shut about me, whoever you are and don't go meddling with my job at the church, or I'll have that ginger scalp of yours for a tea cosy.'

Dizzy and running for the door, Tony gulped in lungfuls of air and flopped down on the pavement. It had started to rain.

*Wow, Mrs Hanks just delivered one whackin' stack of scary news. Wanting to bump me off to say goodbye to their lost boy Victor? Blimey, it's like...it's like Daphne and Terry **were murderers**, or nearly did commit a murder. It's hardly believable.*

Sharp, spiky hammers, gnawed and pounded at

the walls of his skull and a tear swelled and wobbled before it fell. The daylight had gone and the shopping population of Evensham began to blur. Car headlights picked out the slanting raindrops that slipped like spears into the puddles on the pavement.

On the wall beside him a slim plastic box housed a notice board, lit by a tiny blue bulb. Business cards fixed with drawing pins and blotchy with damp advertised the skills of some of the staff at the 'Bar-a-Go-Go'. He couldn't see the cards further up but the bottom one was readable.

Frederick Myatt, it said, Classical Pianist available for christenings, funerals and…

I wonder if he plays the same tunes at all events? Let's see, The Tony Boy's Picnic? If you go down to the waterfall, you're in for a big surprise…

Tony clutched at his fringe and then rubbed his pounding head.

Well, because of Mrs Hanks, now I know. S'ppose I should be grateful to her really.

He scrambled to his feet and studying the notice board again, he saw a small white card, pinned in the centre of the board.

> Get Things Clean and Clear.
> All types of Domestic Work undertaken.
> T. Hanks

Yes, thanks Teresa Hanks, thanks.

Thirty-Seven

Mrs Heapey's room seemed lighter and brighter than usual.

'Have you changed something in here?' he asked, slipping into his chair.

Mrs Heapey smiled. 'We've planned over the last month or so for this to be our last session Tony, and you are leaving Ellodian tomorrow. I guess a lot has changed for you during our time together.'

'A whole bunch of stuff has happened, inside me and out, if you know what I mean?'

'Yes.'

'I can't remember what I've told you and what I've not. I talked to you recently about Daphne and Terry's bonkers murder me plot; their tripped-out solution to losing Victor and their way of saying goodbye. I mean, gruesome. Then I did some thinking, and the "what happened to your mum and dad" question grew two heads.'

'Go on.'

'Mum and Dad, as in Terry and Daphne, died trying to get rid of me, that's what happened to them, but my real mum and dad are out there and I've absolutely no idea where they might be.'

'You seem pretty clear they are together as your parents and are potentially available to you.'

'I suppose I am.'

'An issue for the future maybe?'

'Um.' Tony looked at his hands. 'For now, I think I know who I am, well as much as anyone can. I've also figured out that I wasn't fostered while I was in care because I was nuts. Who wants a child locked in Madsville?'

Tony met Mrs Heapey's steady gaze.

'So, anyhow, I think I've pretty much answered all three questions.'

Mrs Heapey nodded.

'Losing your real parents and finding out your so called 'adoptive' parents wanted to end your life, is traumatic. Very traumatic. If you can bear this news, and learn to live alongside it, you have as good a chance as anybody of living a decent life.'

'Hmm.'

'What is it Tony?'

'Well, it would be tougher if I believed that I'm the only child with parents who wanted to kill me.'

'Say a bit more please.'

'If this was the first time ever, in the history of the world, that a parent wanted to kill their child, then it would feel worse than it does.'

Mrs Heapey blinked.

'But it isn't. I'm not the first. Y'see, when I was out, I rediscovered libraries, not Woosey libraries, real libraries and I had enough time in well mode to read stuff from one or two books. I'm not the only child in history that's been in danger like this. Like I said, gruesome.'

'Gruesome indeed,' said Mrs Heapey.

'I found this lullaby called Rock a Bye Baby. It goes like this:

"Rock a bye baby, in the tree-top.
When the wind blows, the cradle will rock.
When the bough breaks, the cradle will fall.
And down will come baby, cradle and all."

Y'know people actually sing that stuff to their kids. I mean, are they wishing their children dead?'

Mrs Heapey's turquoise eyes remained steady. 'I guess we could read that lullaby as a threat to a child's life, or we could see it as a warning to adults; a message to keep their children out of danger.'

'Hmm, I like the second option best.'

'Me too,' said Mrs Heapey.

'Talking of children in danger, what will happen to Perfax?' Heat crept up his cheeks. 'Perfax did exist, didn't he?'

'He existed for you, in fact…' Mrs Heapey leaned forward, her eyes meeting his. 'Perfax is, or was, quite an important character don't you think?'

'Hmm, I guess. Life in care is lonely. I s'ppose I needed another boy to go through it with me. In my head, Perfax went through it with me. Granted his stuff was a bit different to mine, but like you said, there are similarities.'

'Mmm.'

'Bobbi too and the Cubbages, Gaskin, everybody…' Tony sighed. 'When you say "was", I see I'm not going to meet these people again am I? I mean when I leave? Y'know, now I'm better?'

'They are part of your life and are your memories,' said Mrs Heapey, 'yours to take with you and remember if you want to.'

Tony studied his shoes and then lifting his head absorbed the room, his eyes finally resting on Mrs Heapey.

'Goodbye Tony.'

'I think it is.'

'What's that?'

'A good bye – not a bad bye.'

Thirty-Eight

Climbing on the bus, Tony shifted his rucksack from his back to a seat and sat down.

Do prisoners leaving jail on their release date have this sense of seeing the world, as if for the first time?

Rubbing the window with his sleeve, Tony could see Ellodian, above ground, made of brick and clearly visible from the road.

How long has that car park been there? Those steps and walls and a drive? It's even got massive metal gates. How did I miss those?

Easy Tony, they've always been there, it's just that when you came here...

Yes, I know, thanks Mole; glad you're sticking around.

I'm out of care, can you believe it? I'm out of Ellodian, and away with a little bottle of pills. I've got the address of a new place to stay; they know to expect me, and a meeting with...

He tapped his breast pocket and pulled out a letter.

Bendy Leggett, I'm glad it's her. I must be as ready as I'll ever be.

The little groove in the landscape that marked out the river slowly disappeared from view as the bus rumbled on through the countryside. Over acres of tree-dotted pastureland where Friesian cows grazed, alongside a canal, through grey suburbs with bright graffiti, past rows of neat brick houses, a park with railings and a monochrome high rise, the bus finally juddered to a stop in Evensham's town square.

Tony got off.

Spotting a kiosk that sold coffee, he made his way across the cobbled square. Outside the kiosk, tables and chairs arranged in the shadow of the old town hall awaited the arrival of shoppers.

Two hours before I meet with Bendy.

Inhaling the bright spring morning air, Tony pulled out a chair and sat down. Trees padded with cherry blossom stood out in pastel relief from the flat grey walls of the modern civic buildings. Tugged by the breeze, soft pale blooms fell to the cobbles and rolled this way and that. Shopkeepers materialised from doorways, set out stalls, filled coffee pots, rolled up blinds and began another day. A sense of being new to the world suddenly overwhelmed him.

I'm so, well, on the surface, in the moment and very definitely not underground.

At a nearby table a young woman and her child nursed mugs of chocolate and sang a funny song.

'Was fuzzy Mr Wuzzy dizzy, not fuzzy, was he? Was dizzy Mr Fizzy, fuzzy not dizzy? Was he? I want to know if he's OK and want to know he's here to stay. My friend dizzy Mr Fuzzy, that was he…?'

A man, sitting quietly at the table by his side, wearing a trilby and a large grey overcoat, gave off an air of seriousness. At the next table along, a couple studied a bus timetable and ate bacon sandwiches.

Tony ordered a flapjack and a glass of water. Would McGurney make a landing on the cobbles? Or maybe the Cubbages would pop around the corner and join him for a cup of tea?

These are moments. Moments in time. How is it, that for one moment, a thing can look like one thing, and then a bit later it looks like something else, something completely different? Like Vicky's words at the Sherbets' knock-out tea party.

'It's curious, don't you think, how there are always at least two sides to everyone and two sides at least to everything?'

S'ppose life's full of moments, some good, some bad. I know now that it matters which moments I choose to talk about with others and which moments I should leave – well – to the moment really. It's nearly nine years since my par… – correction, Daphne and Terry – died and since then, it's like moments have rearranged themselves; new worlds have replaced familiar worlds and, I suppose, I've bounded into the landscape of my future. There're some moments I deffo want to forget and some that are absolutely golden, like having tea with the Cubbages. I'll hang on to that forever, and Mrs Heapey, I can't forget her, won't forget her.

How long have I been sitting here? Something could happen right now, and change the moment and doing that, might change the rest of my life.

'One water, one flapjack,' the waitress smiled.

'Thanks.' Tony raised his head. Their eyes locked.

Is she going to say something to me?

The waitress turned away.

Did McGurney actually exist? I've read about lonely children; they make up imaginary friends. Like friends who won't desert them or treat them badly, friends who'll always be there and friends who are much, much better than real live people, any day. And anyway what's real? Real parents, real friends. What's real?

He gave a short snort into his water glass.

The man in the grey overcoat shifted in his chair and looked around. The map reading couple packed up to go. The young woman wiped the chocolate from her child's mouth and two talkative girls with shopping bags sat down at a table opposite.

The town hall clock struck ten

An hour to go before I meet with Bendy Leggett.

Licking the crumbs from his plate, he drank the last of his water and stood up to leave.

The scraping of a chair on cobbles at the next table indicated that the man in the grey coat planned to leave too, but before Tony could take a step, the man moved and blocked his exit. Tony glanced at the trilby-hatted man.

Why couldn't this bloke go the other way 'round the table?

Tony checked his pocket for his wallet.

Is he planning to steal…?

The man moved and stood in front of Tony. As he turned his face, Tony caught sight of his profile.

That eye, it rests at the very outside edge of his round eyelid and that large hooked nose…He's kind of inquisitive.

Hanging back to let him pass, Tony glimpsed the man's grey hair poking out from under his hat. The man stepped ahead and there it was, sticking out from the back vent of his overcoat.

A cherry red tail. Heck! I mean it's a shirt-tail, it's a red tail like Mc…

The bright, vivid colours of the shirt-tail shone unbelievably red against the grey of his coat.

This man's been here since I sat down. **He's been here all along**.

The man moved away.

I even looked at him twice, I could have missed it. It's that eye of his in profile, that eye is deffo, deffo beady.

Goose pimples swept across his skin. In his excitement he almost tripped over the talkative girls' shopping bags and mumbling apologies, loped over to the man, who stood at the back of the queue waiting to pay his bill. The coat was grey and soft; the wool, brushed in one direction, like feathers.

Wow, it would be really fun and friendly to prod him and say something like 'Hello McGurney, pull yer socks up!' That would be cool.

Standing for a moment in the bright morning light, he hesitated. *Perhaps a gentler approach might be better?* Slowly, he lifted his hand to touch the soft grey folds of the coat.

Tony! STOP! Not really McGurney...it's not what you think...only an imaginary comfort...not a parrot, not a parent...Stop stop stop!

Just in time, Tony got the mole's message and pulled his hand away.

Back in the square and momentarily bewildered, Tony could hear someone shouting his name.

'Tony! Tony!'

He swung around.

'Tony, it's you!' Bendy hurried across the square towards him, smiling and loaded up with bags. She tried to free herself and after a bit of juggling, they shook hands.

'I thought it was you. I'm just on my way to Midway House now. How are you?'

'I'm fine,' said Tony.

Thank goodness.

'Good, that's good, would you like a lift?'

———∿∿∿———

Bendy drew up and parked the car outside Midway House. Turning the engine off, she twisted around in her seat to face him.

'Tony, before we go to see your room and before we do anything else, I've got some news.'

His back tightened. 'What is it?'

Calm, calm.

'Are you ready?' said Bendy.

'Yes, but you do realise I know a lot about what happened? I know Daphne and Terry tried to kill me; some crack pot plan to deal with losing Victor, if that's what you're going to say.'

Bendy drew a quick breath. 'Well it's good that you've been able to understand things better and can talk about it. Talking's good. I was going to add a bit, a bit to the jigsaw if you like.'

'Go on then. I'm calm, it's cool.'

'OK. I had a call a few weeks ago from a woman who gave birth to her boy in the maternity wing, when your biological mother was having you. I can't give you her details but the thing is, she left her baby there, she didn't want it. Tony, I think your parents took that abandoned baby home by mistake. I believe this happened because there was a mix-up with cots and wards and well, this is the crucial bit, a mix-up with babies.'

Bendy paused. Tony pushed back his fringe and stared out of the car windscreen.

'Shall I go on?' said Bendy, 'Would you like a minute?'

'Umm, no, it's alright, go on.'

'So, you see, it's looking highly likely that your real parents took home someone else's unwanted baby instead of you. Pretty poor really, I'm so sorry Tony.'

Tony looked at his shoes.

'They thought that baby was me. I did wonder... Could that explain why they never came forward to claim me?'

'Quite possibly. There'll be an investigation, a fact-finding mission is already underway...If at all possible your parents will be located and made aware of what has happened.'

'But how did Terry Jones get hold of me? Mr Burrow who lives on the estate told me that Dad, I mean Terry, worked in the hospital laundry, so how did I get from the ward to the laundry? Or did Terry deliver sheets and stuff to the wards, and swapped me, or stole me – or what?'

He stared hard into Bendy's brown eyes. 'Can we go to the ward?' he said quietly.

'The maternity ward, where you were born?'

Tony nodded.

Bendy checked her watch. 'Go now, you mean?'

'Can we?'

Bendy started the car.

Tony peered through the glass doors.

It's so busy in there and it smells of phenol and cabbage, like the dining room at Daisy Bank. Funny though, somehow that's just a memory now. It doesn't make my heart rattle.

Tony waited on the corridor, while Bendy spoke with a nurse. Through the glass, he could see a nurse at a cot, fixing a name band to an infant's ankle.

So, when Terry got me, however he got me, that plastic name tag read 'Plumb'.

Tony rubbed his nose and stepped back as Bendy came through the door.

'What did you say to the nurse?'

'I spoke to Sister and said you were born here and wanted to see what it was like.'

'Is that all? She'll let me in, based just on that?'

Bendy squared her shoulders. 'That and your pre-nursing studies project.'

'What pre-nursing project?'

Bendy applied a slight pressure to his elbow. 'C'mon,' she said. 'We've only got a few minutes. Do you know what you are looking for?'

Tony shook his head.

Two nurses made up a bed and two more read files in the office. A woman called and one of the nurses making the bed left to attend to her.

'Let's just watch a bit,' said Tony.

The nurse still making the bed bundled up the old laundry, put it temporarily in an adjacent cot, and turned to open a large cotton bag. Then a nurse in blue came and spoke with her and she hurried off. The nurse in blue took over, scooped all the linen from the bed and the cot into the cotton bag, tied it up, opened a metal grille in the wall, hoisted up the bag and pushed it down a chute.

A big blue and white sign hung above the chute.

'LAUNDRY ONLY', it said.

'Nurse, nurse!' The nurse in blue moved away.

'See there, there's another sign taped on below. Let's get closer and see what it says,' said Tony.

In tiny red letters Tony read:

'Check laundry is free from any foreign object before placing in chute.'

Tony looked at Bendy.

'Enough?' she asked.

'Enough.'

—✺—

Turning for the second time that day into the crunchy gravel car park at Midway House, Bendy applied the handbrake and turned to Tony.

'If and when it's possible to contact them, I mean the real ones, your biological parents, I'll be there to help you if that's what you want me to do. There will be checks, assessments, interviews…'

Tony turned his face away.

'Maybe you'll get back to me about that?'

'Mmm…Can I ask you a question?'

'Sure, go ahead.'

'Who paid for me to be at Ellodian? Was it social services?'

'In a way, it was,' said Bendy. Her eyes flicked to the side.

'In a way…?'

'Sometimes rules have to be bent a little, Tony, for things to be possible.'

'So, was it corruption that got me there?'

'No, I don't think it was corruption, but I did bend the rules.'

Tony nodded. 'But nobody was hurt were they, when you bent these rules?' He stole a glimpse into her brown eyes from under his fringe.

'I don't think so,' Bendy sighed. 'Fibbing's wrong, perhaps I shouldn't have, but I guess there's a fine line.'

'Mrs Heapey and I once talked about blame, I was saying something about blaming my mum and dad, you know for what's happened, and I can't remember how we got to it but anyway blame, I've decided, is not good.'

'Right,' said Bendy.

A silence filled the car. Bendy broke it.

'Meantime Tony, I can tell you that I've located your parrot and he's safe. He's been looked after while you've been away, and it's been cleared, you can keep him at Midway. There's a cage and a room that's the right temperature and humidity for him with tree branches and stuff in it, but I expect he'll soon be everywhere he shouldn't be.'

'Did you find McGurney for me, I mean originally, when I told staff at Daisy Bank that I wanted a parrot?'

'No Tony, that wasn't me. Perhaps that's what you were told?'

'It was. Perhaps they didn't want to take the blame for breaking any more rules.'

'Maybe,' said Bendy, 'some adults will tell you anything.'

'True,' said Tony.

'You have to be careful,' they said in unison. Bendy's brown eyes met the clear pale blue of Tony's and the boy and the social worker shared a smile.

Midway House stood big and solid and quite welcoming really. It had a covered porch with scooters, bikes and at least two footballs strewn around the entrance.

'Are you OK to go and see your room and McGurney now?'

McGurney. There, all along.

'Yes,' said Tony, 'yes please.'

Bendy opened the door and climbed out. Tony opened his door but remained in the car. Bendy sauntered around.

'All right Tony?'

'Can I ask another question?'

'Sure, you can.'

Tony stuck one leg out but stayed in his seat. 'Actually, I think I already know the answer, but I'll ask anyway. You didn't send me some hand cream and nail revitaliser, did you?'

'No, I didn't, is that a problem?'

'It never was a problem,' said Tony, 'just a bit weird that's all.'

Bendy nodded.

'C'mon,' said Tony, 'let's go in.'

———∽∾∿∾∽———

Acknowledgements

Anne-Marie Chatwin, Jill Balmont, Shelly Dowd, Martin Roper, Lyn Taylor, Mary Stephenson, Richard and Sarah Urwin, Rosemary and Roger Stephenson, Louise Plant, Gill Lord, Judy Pitt, Sandie Byrne, Ile, Eddie and Katie Ashcroft-Jones, Tog, Louis, Wren, Findlay, Herbie and Beatrice McKenzie, Jenny Maddock, Susanna Geoghegan, Fred and Wendy Oliver, Huw Davis, Esme Towse, Steve Platten, Paddy Acton, Paddy Magrane, Ben Lyte, Sandra Glover, Clare Watson, Steve and Carol Morgan, Cornerstones, The Left Bank and PRS for Music.